Don't dunk your biscuits

For dearest Graham
with many thanks for
your invaluable help and advice.

Don't dunk your biscuits

When you think you're something that you're not

Valerie Broom

BROWN
DOG
BOOKS

First published 2018

Published under licence by Brown Dog Books and
The Self-Publishing Partnership, 7 Green Park Station, Bath BA1 1JB

www.selfpublishingpartnership.co.uk

ISBN printed book: 978-1-78545-267-3
ISBN e-book: 978-1-78545-268-0

Cover design by Andrew Prescott
Internal design by Andrew Easton

Printed and bound by CPI Group (UK) Ltd, Croydon, CR0 4YY

Part 1

Chapter 1

"Tea's ready, Mr Robbins," Lilian called out into the empty bookshop. Lilian's first duty each morning after they had opened up was to brew a pot of 'good Yorkshire tea', as her boss called it. As soon as the tea was brewed to the right degree she poured a strong cup for Albert Robbins and a more milky one with a little sugar for herself.

"Good girl, good girl," smiled Albert as he came into the little storeroom, limping slightly. Lilian had been helping in the shop for a little over a year now and it had proved a most satisfactory arrangement for both.

When Lilian had left school she had thought she might get a job in the nearby town of Market Stamford in a shop or even in a factory like most of her classmates but her mother wouldn't hear of it, insisting that no daughter of hers would do anything "so common" Agnes Woodridge, Lilian's mother, though only the wife of a bank clerk, thought of herself as minor gentry. Lilian and her father, however, gradually managed to convince her mother that if Lilian had a job she could contribute to the housekeeping budget so that they could afford some little luxuries:

"Haddock instead of coley or chops instead of sausages, Mother!"

"Mmm, I was thinking more of some sherry or perhaps a new coat," replied her mother. "Or maybe we could then have the staff for a few more hours," Agnes mused, warming to the idea. 'The staff' was actually just one cleaning lady twice a week but Mrs. Woodridge liked to maintain standards.

Lilian was thrilled when the opportunity to work in the little bookshop came up, for she had loved browsing among the shelves even as a child. Her mother spoke of her job as 'a position' rather than a job and referred to her daughter being a librarian rather than a shop assistant, but no matter, at least she now had a job she enjoyed and some independence.

The shop was invariably empty first thing in the morning so Lilian and Albert Robbins could linger and chat over their cup of tea and a couple of biscuits-- usually Rich Tea, though Lilian couldn't understand why they were called that since they were just about the plainest biscuits you could get; they were lovely dunked into a cup of tea, however, which would never have been allowed at home!

Lilian always enjoyed her chats with Albert very much: he was a knowledgeable and interesting man who held strong opinions but always listening to her views rather than dismissing them, which tended to be the case at home.

Albert Robbins had worked as an estate manager for one of the wealthiest landowners in Scotland before the war. When war was declared Albert joined up at the earliest opportunity, fought in some of the worst campaigns, and was gassed and seriously wounded in trench warfare.

After a long period in hospital he returned to his post on the estate but it was clear that he was never going to be the robust and energetic man he had been before the war. The job was too much for him, but, rather than take a lesser post on the estate, he resigned.

The Laird, a good man though generally taciturn, called him in and insisted on settling a good sum of money on him to set him on his feet again.

Albert had returned to the village where he was brought up, unsure of where his future lay and, as luck would have it, the little bookshop and lending library had recently been put up for sale. He had always enjoyed books and felt he would be able to cope with the quieter way of life so, after some negotiation, he had acquired the lease of the shop and the rather dilapidated stock.

"Did you hear Mr. Chamberlain on the radio last night, Mr. Robbins?" asked Lilian.

"Yes, I did indeed. He spoke quite well, I thought, but there's more to it than meets the eye. Mark my words there's real trouble afoot."

Lilian didn't reply, just sipped her tea and waited; she knew by now when Albert was about to launch into further explanation and she respected his carefully considered and unbiased views.

"You know," he began, "for all the upset and surprise of the abdication, it was really a good thing. If Edward was still King he'd be in the German Chancellor's pocket and our freedom with him."

"Do you think there'll be another war, then?"

"Yes, I do, my dear, and this time it'll come right to our shores."

At that moment the shop doorbell rang, announcing the

arrival of the day's first customer, so Albert rose immediately to greet and serve him while Lilian cleared away the tea things and pondered what she'd just heard.

During the rest of the morning while Lilian dusted, checked shelves and returned books to their correct positions, nearly every customer also had an opinion to voice on Chamberlain and the debates in Parliament and Albert Robbins spent most of the morning leaning on the counter actively encouraging the open exchange of views. Lilian didn't mind at all, she was happiest among the books although she always enjoyed helping readers to choose or to find something appropriate. Several of the ladies from the village enjoyed the same type of novel as she did and they would often compare notes, discuss plots and recommend other titles to one another.

The shop was closed each day for lunch from 1 to 2 o'clock and while Albert heated a can of soup or made a sandwich for himself, Lilian hurried home to a cooked meal. 'Luncheon', as Mrs. Woodridge insisted on calling it, always consisted of a main course and a pudding as it was their main meal of the day. Agnes Woodridge was what is known as a good, plain cook but unimaginative and predictable; so predictable that if you knew what day of the week it was, you knew for sure what was for lunch. Today was Friday so it would be fish of some sort, followed by a rice pudding, which Lilian enjoyed, for she did have a sweet tooth.

The meal was on the table promptly as always and the family sat down to poached smoked cod (known as Golden Fish), boiled potatoes and cabbage.

"Busy at the library today, dear?" asked Mrs. Woodridge.

Ignoring her mother's persistence in pretending the shop was a proper library, Lilian replied, "Yes, quite busy. Mr. Robbins thinks there's going to be another war."

"Stuff and nonsense," replied her mother. "What does he know about it?"

"Well, he studies current affairs a lot."

"Humph, eat your fish."

"I had a rather interesting morning," began Mr. Woodridge, eager to change the subject. "The bank has a new client, a Mr. Blackstock, who's interested in making some investments, and I have been asked to take special care of his account."

"Oh, that sounds good, maybe it'll help with your promotion to Chief Clerk or even Deputy Manager."

"Yes, I hope so, dear. I'll certainly do my best."

"I know you always do your best, Edward. It's really not fair that you've been passed over so many times."

The rice pudding placed in the middle of the table looked delicious with its golden brown crust and a liberal sprinkling of nutmeg. Lilian would have liked a second helping but had to rush to get back to work.

Back at the shop a small parcel of books had arrived by second post so Lilian set to, unpacking and cataloguing before making a little display for the window and shelving the rest in their correct new home. There were few customers during the afternoon, as was often the case at that time, so Lilian was able to make another pot of tea which they both enjoyed whilst reading for a while. Lilian felt herself so lucky to have so much of the world and its stories at her fingertips in this little shop; she often played a game of closing her eyes, reaching out to touch a book randomly to see what new subject or interest she would find in its pages.

Albert kept the shop open each evening until 6 o'clock so that people could call in to browse, buy or exchange books on their way home from work. This was very popular in the village and often proved to be the busiest time of the day. Not so today, however: he was on the point of pulling down the blinds a few minutes early when the door flew open and in rushed Muriel.

Muriel did everything like a whirlwind; she was Lilian's best friend, had been ever since they started at the village school on the same day more than ten years ago. In many ways the two girls were opposites in personality and in looks, perhaps that was why they remained such great friends, complementing each other and rarely quarrelling.

"Hello, Mr. Robbins!" she called, shaking out her blonde curls as she removed a pretty pale blue headscarf.

"Phew, I've run all the way from the bus. I thought I might have missed you."

Albert smiled and nodded. "We'll always wait open for you, my dear, come in." He knew full well that she almost certainly didn't want to borrow a book as she wasn't much of a reader, but she always brought a breath of fresh air and he knew that Lilian was always glad to see her of course. Muriel could have called on her friend later at home but she never felt entirely comfortable with Lilian's parents: she felt she had to be on her best behaviour and talk quietly.

"What's the great hurry, then?" smiled Lilian, sitting her friend down beside the counter.

"I've got some interesting news," Muriel began, taking a deep breath and pausing for effect.

"Well, go on!"

"I've just heard that Stonebury Manor, just down the road, is going to requi---, recer----, taken over by the Army – it's going to be an officers' training camp!! What do you think of that?"

Lilian and Albert glanced at each other, both remembering the talk they'd had just that morning.

"Why is that so interesting?" asked Lilian.

"It's absolutely fascinating – it means there'll be lots of soldiers around."

"Yes, but at the Manor not in the village."

"Ah, but they have to come out sometime and I might meet the man of my dreams!" Muriel placed her hand over her heart, fluttered her eyelashes and pretended to swoon.

All three burst out laughing as she jumped up ready to leave.

"Meet you at the bus stop tomorrow as usual, Lilian."

"Bye, Mr. Robbins." Muriel waved cheerily and was gone.

"That girl's man-mad," muttered Albert, crossing to pull the door blind down and lock up.

Chapter 2

Both girls finished work at lunchtime on Saturdays and it was their practice to meet at the bus stop and take the bus into in to Market Stamford to go window-shopping or maybe go to the pictures. Sometimes they would meet up with some of the other girls from the factory where Muriel worked, but usually it was just the two of them.

Lilian arrived first at the bus stop and ducked into the little bus shelter out of the wind, to wait for her friend. After a few minutes Muriel came running up just as the bus appeared in the distance.

"You're gonna miss this bus one day," Lilian joked.

"No, no – I'm known for my timing. Anyway, I know you'd make him wait for me, wouldn't you?"

As the bus drew up the girls hopped on and made straight for the upper deck; they both loved the view it gave over the fields to open countryside and secretly into small cottage gardens as the bus passed through villages.

In a few minutes the conductor pounded up the stairs to collect fares – it was the regular one with whom they always enjoyed a joke or two. As usual, Muriel was ready with some cheek.

"Two halves, please Mr. Conductor," with a saucy, mock-innocent look on her face.

"Ay, lass, I'm not as green as I'm cabbage looking tha knoous. Town for shopping, is it?" Smiling broadly, he clicked the machine and produced two tickets, full price.

Both girls giggled as he made his way down the bus.

Putting the tickets safely in her bag in case an inspector got on, Muriel turned to Lilian and said, "Now, Lil, you need to put your thinking cap on for me: it's my mum's birthday next week so I'll buy her present today and I haven't got any ideas."

"Okey-dokey, let's have a think. How about a nice box of hankies? They've got some really pretty ones in Marstons."

"I thought about that but I gave her hankies for Christmas didn't I!?"

"So you did, I remember helping you choose them. Well---- I know, your mum makes lovely cakes, doesn't she, so what about a really nice decorated plate to put them on?"

"Oh, that's a brilliant idea, yes," smiled Muriel, warming to the idea. "There's that nice china shop near the bus stop. We'll go there first, shall we? What about you? Have you any shopping to do today?"

"Just a little," replied Lilian. "I need some blue thread from the haberdasher's; I'm putting a velvet collar on my blue dress just to give it a bit of a lift."

"Oh you're so clever. I wish I was handy with a needle, like you." Muriel hadn't the patience to do anything like that and, as she earned more in the factory, she was better able to afford new things than her friend.

"I've also got to call in at the tobacconist's. My father wants some of his special pipe tobacco. The one next to our favourite tea shop keeps it."

"Mmm, I like the smell of your dad's pipe smoke, I wish my dad would change from his old Woodbines."

***

First stop was the china shop where Muriel chose and bought a lovely cake stand decorated with pale blue flowers. The shop assistant wrapped it in tissue paper and put it in a paper bag printed with the shop's name. Muriel was delighted with her purchase.

"That was a good idea of yours, Lil. I'm sure Mum'll like it – we haven't got anything like that at home, it's just like they would have up at the Manor."

"Yes, it's really pretty and you could put a bit of ribbon round the bag – that would look really special."

"Well, yes, I could if I had any ribbon but I haven't."

Lilian thought of suggesting that she buy some in the haberdashery but realised that her friend probably wouldn't care to do that so instead she offered, "If you come indoors when we get back, I'm sure I've got a piece in my workbox you could have."

"Oh O.K. Thanks."

On the way to the haberdasher's the girls enjoyed window-shopping in two or three of the best dress shops in town; Lilian had a good eye and a thrifty frame of mind that made her look and scheme as to the ways she could improvise and improve her own wardrobe, but Muriel simply coveted the smartest, usually most expensive dresses.

There was a bit of a queue in the haberdasher's and by the time Lilian had made her purchase they were more than ready for a sit-down and a cup of tea.

"Let's have tea now," Muriel suggested. "We can get the baccy after – it's just next door."

"Yes, O.K. But don't let me forget it, will you?"

The tea shop on the corner was quite busy but the girls managed to secure their favourite table in the corner of the window. It was the perfect place to enjoy the cosy atmosphere of the café, while being able to see and be seen. On a Saturday afternoon there were usually few young men about: in fact, most would be at football or other hobbies if they weren't working, but any who did pass by got rigorously scrutinised and admired.

"What shall we have?" said Lilian as they sat down and waited for the young waitress to appear.

"Toasted teacake, scone or maybe an éclair?"

"I feel like something a bit different today," replied Muriel. "Éclairs are nice but they're gone in two bites: how about a cream bun?"

"Good idea. Yes, I think today is definitely a cream bun day," laughed Lilian.

As they enjoyed their tea and buns, Muriel couldn't resist reminding her friend about the forthcoming changes at Stonebury Manor.

"Oh yes, I forgot about that," said Lilian. "Are you sure it's true? Who told you anyway?"

"How could you forget about it? It's the most exciting thing that's happened around here. And yes, it's definitely true: Doreen at work told me, I think you met Doreen once when we were queuing at the flicks."

"Yes, I did. She's nice."

"Well, her chap works at the Manor and he told her. It seems the family have to close up part of the house and lock away any private things because the officers will have the run of the rest of the house and grounds."

"Where are the family going to live?"

"They've got to go to their town house which of course is much smaller; so they'll take some staff, but not all. He's worried (Doreen's chap) that he might lose his job and even if he doesn't who's gonna pay him?"

"Yes, must be a worry."

"Well, they were hoping to get engaged at Christmas but Doreen thinks that won't happen now."

"Oh, what a shame."

Muriel took another bite of her luscious cream bun and then continued: "But anyway, isn't it great news for us that there'll be lots of new men around?"

Lilian laughed. "They'll be working and training and IN THE MANOR!"

"Yes, but they've got to come out some time and when they do I'll be there." She fluttered her eyelashes and winked lasciviously. At that both girls dissolved into giggles.

"Just think," Muriel went on, "there might even be one that looks just like Clark Gable – then my future will be decided!"

***

"Hello, Mum, I'm home and Muriel's here," called Lilian as she opened the door and she and her friend stopped a moment in the hall.

"Oh, hello, dear, hello, Muriel." Agnes popped her head around the door of the front room, known in this house as the 'parlour'. The Woodridges were the only people Muriel knew who ever used their front room, except maybe at Christmas.

"How are you, dear?"

"I'm grand, thankee, Mrs. Woodridge. We had a lovely afternoon and we'd tea and cream buns in the café."

"I hope you didn't spoil your teas."

"Oh no, we're growing girls, me and Lil."

"Muriel needs some ribbon so I'm getting her some from my workbox," explained Lilian.

Agnes just nodded as the two girls made their way down to the scullery where Lilian took her workbox down from the dresser. The lilac ribbon was a bit narrow but there was plenty of it so when tied round the parcel and secured with a double bow, it looked fine.

"Oh, that's ever so nice. Thank you, Lil. I'll be off now: see you after church tomorrow?"

"I expect so," replied Lilian, seeing her friend to the door as she called out a cheery goodbye.

"We'll have tea now," Agnes decided, "and then we can settle down for the evening. There's a classical concert on the wireless – it'll be nice to hear some good music."

The music was indeed pleasant as Lilian began to sew the new collar for her dress, but she found her mind going over the afternoon's conversation and Muriel's excitement over the prospect of changes at the Manor. They hadn't, though, talked about the further implications and she wondered just how far-reaching the changes would be to everyone's life if there was a war.

Chapter 3

In Stonebury, as in most parts of the country, the outbreak of war was met with mixed emotions: those who had fresh memories of the last war were anxious and fearful; mothers who had sons of conscription age were worried; some were vaguely annoyed by the inconveniences and challenges to their daily routine, but to many young people, it must be said, it felt like a bit of an adventure.

Every week, it seemed, some new edict or regulation came from central government, ranging from rationing, initially of petrol, then of basic food items, to issue of gas masks and instructions for blackout curtains. People began to plant vegetables where precious rose bushes had been, and new plots were added to the allotment area outside the village.

Mrs. Woodridge found herself approached by members of the Ladies Church Guild to help with the jam-making and fruit bottling; she was glad to share her expertise and in fact became a real leader in the matter of blackout curtains because she had a sewing machine which many households did not possess. Each afternoon for several weeks groups of ladies from the village invaded the Woodridge kitchen to cut and stitch and chat happily. To her surprise Agnes found she made new friends among women she had barely spoken to before.

Lilian's first taste of the effects of wartime came the very first morning after the radio announcement when she arrived at the shop for work to find the door still locked and the blinds down. Albert had always, before, been up and pottering around well before Lilian arrived so, with a little surprise and concern, she tapped on the glass and called out.

After a time she heard him coming down the stairs from his flat, calling out, "Sorry, dear, got up a bit late."

"Not to worry," replied Lilian as she took off her jacket and went straight away to fill the kettle.

It was in her mind to ask her boss if he had heard Mr. Chamberlain's announcement, but one look at Albert's dishevelled appearance and the haunted, fearful look on his face told her he definitely had. She knew only that he must have had a bad time in the First World War, resulting in having to give up the career he had loved, but the extent to which the memories still affected him she could only guess at. She was very fond of Albert and judged the best thing to do was just make the tea and chat as normal. He seemed to calm down and admitted to Lilian that he'd had a bad night and some bad dreams. In fact the truth was that he'd been experiencing some flashbacks for some time as the threat of war had increased, but the speech declaring war seemed to have sprung a switch in his mind and the nightmares that pursued him were unbelievable.

Everyone who came into the shop had but one topic of

conversation and that just the topic Lilian and Albert were trying to avoid. Every time the door opened and at the slightest noise in the shop Albert jumped as though his nerves were shot. The worst incident came during the afternoon when two lads from the village came in to purchase some stationery; both of them were full of the news of war and of their intentions to join up as soon as possible, the younger one even planning to lie about his age so he could join up sooner.

Albert got so agitated, Lilian had never seen him so angry, actually she'd never seen him angry at all – he was generally such a mild and gentle man.

"Don't you dare! You silly little fools. Don't join up a moment before you have to – that'll come soon enough. It's insanity to want to go to war – you think you're gonna be heroes – you're more likely to be dead or worse. And think about your poor parents – think how they'll feel."

Albert paused for breath, breathing heavily and visibly shaking. The lads were not a little shocked by this outburst and in the spirit of their warlike intentions, prepared to back up their ideas, but a tiny shake of the head by Lilian quelled them and they completed their purchase and left, mumbling a bit.

During the rest of the day Albert became more and more withdrawn and morose, even though Lilian did her best to keep cheerful and lighten the atmosphere. She knew he hadn't eaten anything all day so just before closing time she asked, "What are you going to have for your tea, Mr. Robbins?"

"Oh, I might just have a bit of toast," he replied.

"Why don't I make you some scrambled eggs before I go? Have

you got some eggs?"

"Yes, I think so. Mrs. Watson along the road keeps me supplied from her few chickens in the backyard."

Not waiting for any further reply she busied herself preparing the eggs and set them for Albert to eat in the little storeroom.

"Thank you, my dear. What a good girl you are," said Albert with a gentle smile.

"Oh, it's nothing, Mr. Robbins. Now I must be off, Mother will wonder where I am. See you tomorrow!"

Grabbing her coat, she almost ran out of the door and hurried home because it was a fact that if she was ever late returning home she could expect some sort of sarcastic remark from Agnes.

Albert, for his part, tried to eat some of the little meal but only managed a few mouthfuls before the blackness he had been fighting all day overcame him. Pushing the plate away, he leaned forward with his head in his hands and closed his eyes, only to snap them open a few minutes later and say aloud, "My God, I'm afraid to sleep."

Lilian arrived home slightly breathless and with cheeks pink from the cool breeze. Letting herself into the hall and hanging up her jacket, she heard her mother call, "Hello, dear, we're in the parlour."

Lilian immediately knew there must be a guest, for Agnes had used her 'visitors' voice'. Entering the parlour she saw there was indeed a gentleman visitor comfortably reclining in an armchair and drinking sherry, which usually only happened at Christmas in the Woodridge house.

"Ah, Lilian, home at last. I'd like you to meet Mr. Blackstock –

he's a friend of Father's from the bank."

"Hello," replied Lilian. "Sorry I'm late, I stayed on a bit because Mr. Robbins hadn't been too well."

"Oh, well, never mind. Your tea's in the oven – we've had ours earlier."

"Thank you, Mother."

As Lilian left to fetch her meal she heard Agnes explaining about her daughter's 'position' and how she was relied on a great deal in the library. She couldn't help smiling at the way her mother always exaggerated such things. The cottage pie that was her tea was rather dried up, so Lilian made a cup of tea to go with it and was rather glad to hear cordial "Goodbyes" as the visitor departed.

Next morning the shop was again all locked up when Lilian arrived for work and she waited even longer for Albert to appear. He was again very apologetic to have kept her waiting but she made light of it. Albert in fact stayed in the back room much of the day and Lilian was glad about that because she saw several military vehicles heading to the Manor, fearing that the sight of them would make him feel even worse.

Each day now Albert was becoming more and more withdrawn so that Lilian was almost running the store and the library, apart from the money side of things. She didn't mind at all doing extra work while her boss spent most of the day reading his favourite poems and mouthing the long passages that he had memorised. Poetry was his solace.

Towards teatime next afternoon the shop bell rang and a smart, young private marched in. "Good afternoon," called Lilian, glancing across to see how Albert would greet the young man, concerned in case the uniform upset him. Albert just nodded, seeming at the moment to be miles away in a world of his own.

Although in her private life Lilian would never be one to start conversations with strangers, she had found that in the shop she seemed to assume a different persona and was always ready to engage with customers and advise them on their choices.

"How can I help you?" she immediately asked the soldier.

"Oh thank you, Miss. I'm from the Manor down the road and Captain Doyle has asked me to pick up a couple of books for him – if you have them in stock."

So saying, he handed Lilian a folded piece of paper with the titles and authors neatly prescribed.

"I think we have both of these," answered Lilian. "They'll be in that section over there. If you need any help give me a call."

The young man found the books easily but then spent quite some time browsing. Lilian supposed he was glad to be away from the regimentation of Army life for a time.

Approaching the counter, he asked, "You lend books as well here, then, do you?"

"Oh, yes, you can borrow something if you wish. There's just a small fee and you'd need to fill in one of our cards."

"I'll do that then, if I may."

After filling out the form and paying Albert the required sum, he gathered up the books and turned to Lilian. "Thank you so much for your help. This is a lovely little shop. Good afternoon."

Lilian blushed a little at the compliments and replied, "Goodbye. I do hope you enjoy the book."

Later that afternoon, Muriel paid one of her flying visits, bursting in the door with a flurry of autumn leaves behind her.

"Shut the door behind you, young lady," growled Albert.

"Sorry, Mr. Robbins."

"What's up with him?" Muriel mouthed to her friend.

"I'll tell you later."

"Oh, O.K. Well guess what, guess what?"

"What?" replied Lilian, suspecting she might know what was coming next by the excited look on the girl's face.

"Doreen says the first group of officers have arrived at the Manor and her chap's having to help sort the place out, proper spring cleaning and all. So I reckon they must be getting ready for a party."

"Oh, Muriel, they're here to train not to give parties, and actually I saw the trucks come through a couple of days ago."

"Yes, but they've got to have some relaxation: they can't train all the time."

"No, I suppose not. There was a young soldier in here this afternoon picking up some books for his captain."

"Whaaaat!! Why didn't you tell me?"

"I just did."

"What was he like? Was he really handsome? How tall is he??"

"He was just ordinary really – quite nice."

"QUITE NICE!!! Oh Lilian, you're hopeless. If he comes in again, find out his name and if he's got a friend."

"Oh he will be coming in again to return the book he borrowed."

"He borrowed a book!! Oh he's an intellectual. I do love an intellectual."

So saying, Muriel executed one of her pretended swoons and hurried off home, leaving her friend smiling at her nonsense.

Chapter 4

Still smiling at her friend's irrepressible optimism, Lilian tidied up, filing away the card that the young soldier had filled in, noticing that his name was Michael Baxter. Mmm, nice name, she thought: suits him somehow.

Window-shopping at the present time seemed frivolous somehow so Muriel and Lilian queued for the Picture House, hoping to see one of their screen heroes. Muriel still kept on about how disappointed she was that she had not seen any of the military personnel from the Manor.

"What's the good of having a load of officers training nearby if they're always stuck behind high walls?"

"Mmm, well, if something doesn't happen soon I might have to take drastic action."

Both girls laughed as they imagined what that might be and moved along towards the opened doors of the cinema.

The main film was a light musical comedy, the second feature a Gothic piece about a haunted castle, and there was of course the Pathé News, the main feature of which was about the 'evacuees' from London's East End: crocodile rows of mixed ages from 3 to 13 with their gas masks and parcels containing some spare clothes. Some of the youngsters appeared to be quite nonchalant about the whole affair, but others were in tears and looking very lost.

On the way home it was clear that the children had affected Muriel and Lilian much more than the films. Muriel was the first to speak. "I do feel sorry for all those little 'uns having to be shipped off to goodness knows where. I'm really glad none of our little 'uns will have to go away."

Muriel was the eldest of five children so their home was full to bursting and her parents were very glad of the wages she bought home from the factory.

"You've got a spare room, though, haven't you, Lil? So you might get some kids billeted on you. From what the film said it doesn't seem as if you get any choice in the matter. What would your mum say about that?"

"Oh, she'd be alright. She's quite fond of children, actually."

Muriel didn't say anything but she was thinking that any evacuees in Agnes Woodridge's care would certainly have to "mind their p's and q's".

Private Baxter returned to the bookshop a few days later, again with two missions to carry out. As the shop bell rang Lilian looked up with her ready smile.

"Good morning, Mr. Baxter," she began.

"Good morning, Ma'am. You remembered my name! But it's Private Baxter, please, since I joined up."

"So sorry, I'm not used to military titles yet, Private Baxter." This was said a bit tongue-in-cheek and both laughed.

"Have you come to return your book? Did you enjoy it?"

"Yes, on both counts but I have another message to do for Captain Doyle and I wondered if you could help?"

"Certainly if we can," smiled Lilian.

"Captain Doyle's asked me to put this notice up in the village hall," Michael began, unrolling a large printed sheet and holding it up for Lilian to read. It was an invitation for the whole village to an Open Afternoon and Tea Dance at the Manor.

"Oh that's really nice," said Lilian. "Muriel will be pleased."

"Muriel?" wondered Michael, looking puzzled.

"Oh, it doesn't matter. But why do you need our help?"

"Well, I need to know who to see to get permission to put up the notice where most people would see it."

Albert looked up from his book and gruffly interposed. "You'll need to speak to the verger, young man, because it'll need to go on the noticeboard in the church hall, we don't have a village hall as such."

"Thank you, sir. Where will I find him?"

"Runs the post office just down the road, easy to find."

"Thank you very much again, I'll do that just as soon as I've found another book to borrow."

Lilian carried on tidying some of the shelves as Michael picked up a book here and there. Seeing him open a large, classic volume, she asked, "Do you get much time for reading up at the Manor?"

"No, actually very little as a rule, but now and then there's a lull and I do love to read when I can."

"Me, too, I read every night before bed and sometimes in the day if we're not too busy."

At length, Michael selected his book, signed the card and paid the small fee. On his way out he said, "I do hope you'll both be able to come up to the Manor. I think you'll find it interesting."

"Maybe," replied Albert non-committally.

"I'll see," said Lilian, not meaning to be coquettish but genuinely because, as quite a shy girl, she didn't usually enjoy meeting strangers. On the other hand, she had a feeling that as soon as Muriel found out about the social she would definitely be dragged along with her.

Arriving home after work that day, Lilian found the house was empty and a note on the kitchen table from her mother.

"Gone to a meeting of the Evacuation Committee, cold meat in the larder."

Lilian had never heard of the Evacuation Committee but supposed it had to do with those poor city children that she and Muriel had talked about. As she put together some ham and pickles for her tea she reflected how quickly the war had affected even their quiet village.

An hour or so later Agnes returned, asking Lilian to put the kettle on as soon as she had hung up her hat and coat.

"Goodness me, some people do like to hear themselves talk," remarked Agnes. "I thought I'd never get away – we could have been done in half the time if Reverend Jones hadn't kept on and on."

Lilian smiled at the reference to their talkative clergyman and asked, "What was the meeting about then?"

"We're organising billets for evacuated children from Merseyside. I'm going to co-ordinate and check all the arrangements for this side of the village."

Agnes visibly preened, obviously relishing the responsibility she had been given.

"We shall have to take at least one evacuee ourselves as we've got a spare room. I hope you don't mind, Lilian?"

"Of course not, Mother. We saw pictures of the children at the Gaumont, poor little souls, some really small."

"Tomorrow I'll spring-clean the spare room so that it's all ready. We're expecting the first group in a day or two."

"I'll give you a hand after work, if you like."

"Thank you, dear."

They stayed in the kitchen for a while drinking their tea until Agnes looked up at the clock and said, "I thought your father would have been back by now – he was meeting Mr. Blackstock after work. They do seem to be getting on so well and he's such a nice man."

Lilian found she was actually looking forward to having a child in the house.

She looked out some of her old toys and favourite children's books, thinking it might make the newcomer feel more at home.

In the event Lilian's things were not much use because the child that came home with Agnes a few days later was a scrawny young lad about ten years old. Agnes brought him home with her after the first group of children had arrived and been allocated.

"Hang your coat up there, Tom, and come and meet Lilian, my daughter."

The lad shuffled into the kitchen looking very unsure of himself.

"Hello, dear, this is Tom. I'm sure he'd like a cup of tea and I know I would."

Lilian turned to smile at the boy, understanding that he must feel very shy.

"Hello, Tom. It's nice to meet you. I bet you'd like a piece of cake as well, wouldn't you?"

Tom mumbled some sort of reply and sat down at the kitchen table where he was told and in a few moments a cup of strong tea and a large slice of cherry cake were put in front of him. He immediately took a large bite of cake and began to eat with great concentration. It was the most delicious cake he'd ever had; his mum sometimes bought lardy cake from the baker's, but usually they had only had bread and dripping or a scrape of jam.

"It's smashing cake, Missus," he said as he finished and licked his fingers.

"I'm glad you like it, Tom, but you must call me Mrs. Woodridge."

"Yes, Missus."

Agnes rolled her eyes and shrugged before asking Lilian to show Tom where his room was and where he could wash.

"Come on, Tom. This way – bring your things."

The boy's only luggage, apart from his gas mask, was a small bundle tied up in what appeared to be sackcloth.

Upstairs Lilian opened the door of the small spare room.

"Here you are, this is your room. I hope you like it."

Tom took in the tidy little room containing just a single bed, a chest of drawers and one chair.

"Do you mean this is only for me?" he asked.

"Yes, of course. I've got my own room and my parents have theirs. Why don't you put your clothes in the drawers, then come down? There's some soup for our evening meal a bit later."

Lilian had made leek and potato soup and Agnes was mashing it down to make it as smooth as possible when Tom came back down to the kitchen. Edward glanced up from his paper and beckoned the lad forward, introducing himself and chatting to help him feel more at home.

The table was soon laid with bowls of soup and fresh, crusty rolls from the bakery. Tom looked at his soup uncertainly – it was quite green – but after the first spoonful found it tasted really good. In fact he was enjoying it quite a lot and slurping rather loudly. Lilian and her father looked at each other, suspecting there would be a comment, and sure enough:

"Tom, try to eat your soup more quietly please."

"Yes, Missus."

It actually made little difference and it was clear the boy had enjoyed the meal as he wiped the last drops of soup up with his roll. Without being asked he helped clear the table, earning approval all round. It wasn't long before it was clear Tom was ready for bed; it had been a long, stressful day.

"Seems a nice enough lad," Edward remarked when Tom had left the room.

"Well, his table manners leave a lot to be desired but that's only to be expected, I suppose," replied his wife.

All was soon quiet and when the family turned in, Agnes peeped in to see Tom fast asleep with his clothes neatly folded on the chair. She nodded her approval.

Around midnight there was suddenly an anguished cry, "Let me out, let me out!" and a great crashing down the stairs.

"What on earth was that?" cried Agnes.

"I'll go, dear," said Edward, stepping into his slippers.

At the bottom of the stairs he found Tom in his underwear, wide-eyed and shivering.

"I thought I was locked in – I thought I was in prison."

Edward realised they must have shut the bedroom door, not knowing that the lad was used to little privacy.

"There now, you're alright. Let's get you back to bed and we can leave your door open."

Agnes had heard the exchange and only said, "I hope he didn't wake Lilian," when Edward got back into bed.

"It's bound to take a while for him to settle. He'll be alright. Goodnight, dear."

***

Lilian was quite right about Muriel's reaction to the open invitation to the Manor. Her eyes were shining and she looked as if she'd explode as she bubbled over telling her friend all about the notice on the church hall board.

"Yes, I know, actually, Private Baxter showed me the poster in the shop."

"You knew! Why didn't you tell me? Lilian, you are the living end but never mind, isn't it great news? We'll go together and we'll make sure we look our best."

"I don't think I really want to go, Muriel. You know I'm not very comfortable with strangers and I can't dance very well."

"Lilian Woodridge, if you don't come with me, I'll never speak to you again! You must come."

Lilian sighed, knowing she couldn't really get out of it. "Alright, alright, if it's so important to you."

"Good. That's settled. Now, what shall I wear?"

Chapter 5

In point of fact neither of the girls had much choice in the matter of what to wear for the social occasion but it was fun to discuss the merits of one outfit or another and to try their hair in a more up-to-date style. Lilian had wondered if her parents might object to her attending the social but they raised no objection, both of them at the same time quite busy with their own work – Edward at the bank and Agnes in her new role of Evacuee Co-ordinator, something Lilian could never have imagined her doing.

Muriel was to call for Lilian on the way to the Manor at just about 2 o'clock so that they wouldn't be the first to arrive. The walk up to the Manor was really pleasant, a dry day and quite warm – bit of an Indian summer really.

"How're you getting on with the lad you've got staying, Lil?" asked Muriel.

"Tom! Oh, he's fine really; obviously it's taking him a bit of time to get used to us and to being in the countryside. I think he was quite homesick at first but he gets on quite well with Father and he's certainly got a good appetite."

"Eating you out of house and home, is he? Boys that age are always hungry – I know from ours at home. Has he made any new friends?"

"Yes, he and his pals are always out and about, building dens and suchlike. He seems to get on really well with most people – all except Mr. Blackstock. Whenever he comes to the house Tom disappears."

"Who's Mr. Blackstock?"

"He's a sort of client of Father's from the bank. I'm not really sure why he's here so often but apparently he's quite important."

A few other villagers were walking the same way and they arrived at the Manor gates just behind a family with two small children. As they passed the soldier on guard at the gate Muriel smiled and winked saucily, where upon the man saluted equally saucily. Lilian shook her friend by the arm and hissed, "Muriel, don't."

As they walked up the gravel path to the house the grounds still looked splendid: hoops for croquet were laid ready on the lawn, the sun was glinting on the lake beyond, and there was already a group playing tennis on the court behind the house.

"It's lovely here, isn't it?" sighed Lilian.

"Mmm," murmured Muriel, already on the lookout for men.

The door of the house stood open to welcome guests and in the hallway two young privates were helping people to hang up their jackets before they proceeded to the drawing room.

Captain Doyle was near the doorway greeting visitors.

"Good afternoon, ladies. How nice of you to come. I do hope you enjoy the afternoon. There's tea and biscuits just over there if you would like."

"Thank you, sir," replied both girls, moving on to let the next group through.

"Cor, he's a bit of alright," whispered Muriel.

"Tut, Muriel, he's obviously the officer in charge and he's probably married."

Muriel winked again. "Doesn't mean he's not dishy."

Tea and biscuits were obtained and girls looked around in wonder really at the size of the room. It wasn't elegantly furnished as it would have been when the family were there but it was still a lovely room with views out across the lake.

Muriel brazenly walked up to a small group of young soldiers, saying, "Come on, Lil, we came to meet chaps, didn't we?"

Her friend hung back, though, and as soon as she could she wandered over to the window to enjoy the view. A few moments later she felt a tap on her shoulder and turned to see Michael smiling broadly and greeting her:

"Hello there – I'm so glad you could come. Do you remember me?"

"Of course I do – Private Baxter, isn't it!?"

Lilian was secretly delighted to see his friendly face.

"Michael is my name; I think we're well enough acquainted for first names but I don't know yours."

Lilian told him and they shook hands rather formally. Michael asked if she'd come alone, really fishing to see if she had a boyfriend.

"No, I came with my friend Muriel – that's her over there."

Muriel was already surrounded by a small group of soldiers and was clearly flirting with more than one of them.

Just at that moment someone set a gramophone playing dance music and almost immediately Muriel was on the dance floor with the shortest of her admirers, who turned out to be an excellent dancer. In no time at all they were executing a very exuberant foxtrot.

"I would ask you to dance," said Michael to Lilian, "but I usually like to wait until the floor is a bit more crowded – if you know what I mean."

"Yes, I'm the same. Let's wait a bit," replied Lilian.

Glancing out of the window, Michael had an idea: "Would you like a game of croquet instead?"

"Well, I've never played croquet before but I don't mind giving it a go!"

"Come on, then. We'd better collect your jacket: you might need it outside."

Once on the lawn they collected mallets and balls whilst Michael briefly explained the object of the game. He showed Lilian how to hold the mallet and they set off at a cracking pace. The first two hoops were quickly passed but as the lawn sloped away and Michael's deliberately obvious attempts to cheat became more outrageous, they were soon laughing helplessly and enjoying each other's company enormously. After the game they returned the equipment to the box but were loath to go back inside just yet. The laughter and exercise had put a glow on Lilian's cheeks and a sparkle in her eyes. Michael thought how pretty she looked and suggested a stroll around the lake.

As they walked he asked about Albert, having realised that he hadn't seemed very well. Lilian explained that he was of a nervous disposition and people thought it might be to do with the experiences and injuries he suffered in the last war.

"The poor chap probably had shell-shock, you know, and they say some people never get over that."

"What would happen to the bookshop if he couldn't keep on with it?"

"Well, I think I could manage it if he wanted me to; I know all about the day-to-day running and ordering."

Lilian was quiet for a while, thinking how Albert did seem to be deteriorating day by day. Until now she hadn't really allowed herself to consider the possible consequences, but talking about it had brought her vague concerns to a focus.

The light was fading as they strolled back towards the house and a cool breeze was getting up.

"I'd better be getting home," said Lilian. "I'll need to start the tea."

"Of course. May I walk you home?"

"Thank you. That would be nice."

They walked slowly along the darkening lanes, not touching but close together and not wanting to part. They talked about their favourite books and music they both enjoyed, finding they had so much in common.

At the garden gate they still stood talking for a few minutes until with a great crash and bump Tom came careering down the opposite bank and almost knocked them both over.

"Sorry, Lil. Sorry, sir!" he called out as he disappeared, running round to the back door.

"Wow," laughed Michael. "Was that your brother?"

"No," smiled Lilian, "that's Tom – he's our evacuee from the city."

"He seems a bit wild."

"No, not really; he's just really enjoying the freedom of the countryside, I think."

"I must go in now, Michael. Thank you for walking me back – I had a really nice afternoon."

"So did I – may I see you again? Would you come out with me next Saturday?"

Lilian hesitated only a moment before saying, "Yes, I'd like to."

"Brilliant. Shall I call for you at about 2 o'clock?"

"Umm, I think it might be better if I meet you at the corner by the bookshop, if that is O.K."

"Alright – it's a date. Bye for now."

So saying, he leaned forward and kissed Lilian lightly on the cheek. Taken by surprise, she found her heart was fluttering as she watched him march off down the lane, whistling and waving.

Tom was in the kitchen munching an apple. Grinning at Lilian he asked, "Is that your sweetheart?"

"No, he's just a friend."

"Looked like a sweetheart to me," muttered the lad.

Lilian aimed a playful slap at him, but he ducked and asked, "Can I have a biscuit?"

"Course you can – if there are any in the tin."

"I'll just have the broken ones. That'll be alright, won't it?"

"I should think so."

As Tom turned his back to her to replace the biscuit tin Lilian noticed several long threads hanging from a rip in his jumper.

"How did you tear your jumper, Tom?"

"Oh, I caught it on a branch when we were mending the roof of the den. It's alright."

"It's not alright. If it's not fixed it'll just get bigger and Mother won't be too pleased. Come on, we'd better get a needle and do a running repair before she gets home."

"Thanks, Lil. You're a pal."

Chapter 6

Just as Lilian and Edward arrived at the lych-gate leading into the churchyard, Muriel came running up to greet them:

"Good morning, Mr. Woodridge. Hello, Lil. Lovely morning, isn't it?"

Edward raised his hat, smiled and nodded but walked on, leaving the two girls to chat for a minute.

"I'm glad I've seen you, Muriel – would you come to give me a hand making the tea after church 'cos Mother hasn't come – she isn't feeling too great this morning."

"Course I will – give us a chance to have a chat about yesterday. Wasn't it great?"

Lilian flushed a little and smiled but didn't answer because they'd arrived at the pew where her father was sitting with head bowed. She slipped in beside him and squeezed up so Muriel could sit there, too. Seeing him a little surprised, she whispered, "Muriel's going to help me with the tea later."

Edward nodded and smiled at Muriel gratefully. Just recently he had been rather concerned that his wife was taking on a bit too much, especially in the area of overseeing the placements of evacuees; he had even mentioned his concerns to his friend Desmond (Blackstock) when they were having a quiet drink in the village pub. Desmond's attitude had been quite reassuring and indeed he had waxed quite lyrical in his praise of the charms of both Agnes and Lilian, with the result that Edward felt such a glow of pride that he picked up their empty glasses and returned to the bar for refills although it really wasn't his round. Funny thing, that – although Desmond always seemed affluent he always managed to avoid buying a round. No, thought Edward, that's an uncharitable thought, especially here in church, so he pushed such a mean idea away and concentrated on the positive thought that a little rest for his wife today would do her the world of good.

Directly after the Communion part of the service the two girls slipped out of the side door and hurried across to the church hall to get kettles on and the crockery laid out. Lilian reached down for the big, brown enamel teapots and got the tea caddy out of the cupboard while Muriel started laying out the cups and saucers on a long table.

"What did you think of the 'do' yesterday, then?" asked Muriel. "I danced so much I was exhausted when I got home. I saw you talking to that chap by the window; didn't he ask you to dance?"

"That was Michael, the soldier who came into the shop last week. He asked me to play croquet instead, so we did that and then went for a walk around the lake."

"Played croquet – wow! – that's rather posh!"

"Not really but it was fun."

"What happened to you after that? I looked for you so we could walk back together but I couldn't see you."

"Oh sorry, Muriel, but Michael asked to walk me home and I said yes."

"I bet you did! Well – well, tell me more. What's he like? Are you seeing him again?"

"He's really nice, actually. We chatted about all sorts of things and I'm meeting him on Saturday."

"Lilian Woodridge, you are such a dark horse. There's me thinking you might have gone home early and in fact you've gone and got off with a fella and now you've got a date!"

At that moment the vicar's wife bustled in carrying a large biscuit tin.

"How are you getting on? Oh you're nearly ready, thank you so much. I've brought some biscuits but I don't know how much longer we'll be able to have biscuits, what with the rationing."

Muriel opened the tin of biscuits and began to arrange them on a plate while Lilian and Mrs. Smythe warmed the teapots and made the tea. By the time the parishioners wandered in the tea was nicely brewed and the teacups ready milked.

The villagers mingled and chatted over their tea but there was little small talk or weather remarks as there would have been just a few weeks ago: some talked about yesterday's social at the Manor; almost everyone knew about a husband, brother or son who had been called up or some that would soon be enlisting; there were also rumours, as yet unconfirmed, that Land Army girls were to be billeted in or near the village to maximise food production in the area.

Lilian and Edward didn't stay long, conscious that Agnes

hadn't been too good earlier, and neither did Muriel, for she always helped her mum prepare a proper Sunday lunch, a family tradition that was not to be allowed to lapse.

Much to their surprise on arriving home, the Woodridges found Agnes and Tom in the parlour engrossed in a game of draughts. Agnes was looking much better and the delicious aroma of roast chicken was emanating from the kitchen.

"You look better, dear," said Edward, patting Agnes' shoulder, "and you managed to get the lunch on!"

"Oh yes – I had a lot of help." She smiled across at Tom, who looked up and proudly said, "I did all the spuds and the carrots."

"Well done, lad."

"There's only the cabbage and the gravy to do, Lilian. Could you do that while we finish our game?"

"Of course, and I'll make a semolina pudding that's quick and it's nice with a dollop of jam."

"Mmm, that's me favourite," grinned Tom.

"Everything's your favourite," smiled Lilian, noticing not for the first time how the lad had filled out in the short time he'd been with them.

"You've got hollow legs, you have!"

***

Friday evening and Muriel had popped in for a chat. After making a cup of tea and buttering some scones, the girls took the snack up to Lilian's room.

"Are you nervous?" asked Muriel.

Knowing that her friend referred to her forthcoming 'date' with Michael, Lilian replied, "No, why should I be nervous? But I am quite excited, and sometimes I get butterflies when thinking about meeting him."

"Thought so!" said her friend. "Now what are you going to wear? You wore the blue dress on Saturday so you can't wear that again. Anyway, where's he taking you?"

"I don't know, p'raps we'll just go for a walk or maybe the pictures."

Muriel went across to the small wardrobe and threw it open. "This skirt's nice," she said, holding a dark green tweed. "What have you got that goes with it?"

"The best is the Fair Isle jumper Mother made me for Christmas."

"Oh yes, that really suits you – That'll be perfect. Now what about your hair!? Sit down!"

With much giggling and joking, the two friends spent nearly an hour trying out different styles on each other's hair, finally settling on a style for Lilian which pinned the side and front hair into neat rolls and was much more sophisticated than her usual casual waves.

"It looks good but I don't think I can do it myself," she said.

"You'll just have to practise. Hey, look at the time – I must be going. Have fun tomorrow and be good!"

Laughing and winking, Muriel ran down the stairs, calling out her farewells.

***

Michael was already waiting on the corner when Lilian hurried along the road and his face lit up as soon as he saw her.

"Hello, I hope I'm not late."

"No, not at all. I was a bit early. I thought we could get the bus into town. Is that alright?"

"Yes that's fine."

They didn't have to wait long and they were soon settled onto the upper deck. Michael paid their fares. It wasn't the regular conductor, for which Lilian was grateful, as she had feared he might make some cheeky comment. At first they sat in silence feeling a little awkward but then both started to speak at the same moment which made them laugh and the awkwardness disappeared.

In town they strolled along the river and after a few minutes Michael took her hand. She smiled up at him and squeezed his hand; it felt just right.

On the way back towards the town centre Michael suggested that they get some afternoon tea, to which Lilian readily agreed: "A sit-down and a cup of tea would be most welcome." She expected they'd go to the café on the corner or the tea shop further down but they carried on past both establishments until they reached the Stamford Grange Hotel. As they mounted the steps Michael explained, "A very special lady like you deserves a very special afternoon tea!"

Lilian smiled and continued up the steps but began to feel nervous – was her hair still tidy? Was she dressed smartly enough? She had only been to a hotel once before when a distant cousin of her mother's got married, but Agnes had been in a state of high agitation for days beforehand, issuing instructions on etiquette and decorum.

She needn't have worried, the atmosphere was totally relaxed and welcoming. Michael approached the reception and asked if they could order 'afternoon tea', whereupon the friendly receptionist replied, "Of course, sir. If you'd like to take a seat in the lounge I'll send someone to take your order right away."

The hotel lounge was a delightful room, the perfect blend of cosy and luxurious, with sumptuous sofas and a glowing open fire. The large windows looked out onto a well-kept lawn where croquet hoops had been planted.

"Look at that, Lilian. They must have known that two croquet champions were coming to tea!"

They both laughed, remembering what fun they had playing the game last week, and found a seat near the window.

The afternoon tea was superb: served on a tall cake stand, there were tiny salmon and cucumber sandwiches, fresh scones with cream and jam, and two types of cake – meringues and fairy cakes. All washed down with a generous pot of tea, it made a really lovely treat and the young couple did it justice.

"No rationing here yet, then," sighed Lilian, as they enjoyed the last of the tea.

They carried on chatting about anything and everything until Lilian, glancing out of the window, noticed the shadows forming and realised it must be getting late.

"I'd better be going," she said. "Mother will wonder where I am."

"Yes, of course. I'll just go and pay the bill, then we'll get the bus. Don't want you to get into trouble."

They didn't have to wait long for the bus and they held hands all the way home. At the garden gate Michael said, "I don't know when I can get off next week so can I get a message to you at the shop?"

"Yes, that'll be O.K. Thank you for a lovely afternoon."

Smiling gently, he reached out to push back a curl that had escaped its grip and stroking her cheek he bent to kiss her lips. This time it was a long, lingering embrace that took her breath away. Reluctantly they parted and Lilian ran up the garden path before turning to wave goodbye.

Opening the door, she called out, "Hello! Sorry I'm late." Her parents were in the parlour where Edward was busy tuning the wireless for the nightly ritual of listening to the News.

"Your tea's keeping warm in the stove, dear. Thought you'd got lost," huffed Agnes.

Tom came down the stairs and accompanied Lilian into the kitchen.

"It's sausage and mash tonight," he said. "It were really nice."

Quietly closing the door, Lilian turned off the gas and put the hot plate on the table before turning to Tom, saying, "I'm not really hungry, Tom. Could you help me with this? I don't want it to go to waste."

The lad's reaction was predictably a wide grin and a vigorous nod of the head. She watched him tuck in before saying, "Make sure you clear up, won't you?"

"Will do, thanks, Lil."

"Don't call me Lil. You know Mother doesn't like it."

"Sorry, Mistress Lilian," he cheekily retorted and added, "but I know why you're not hungry!"

Lilian ignored his cheek and made her way up to her room wondering how it was that Tom did always seem to know more than what was good for him!

In her room she lay down, fully clothed, on the bed, thinking back on the events of the afternoon and mentally hugging herself with happiness. At one point she got up and looked in the mirror to see if she looked different because she certainly felt different.

Chapter 7

Lilian was pleasantly surprised on Monday morning when she arrived at work because Albert seemed a little better. The shop door was unlocked, he was pottering about and had even put the kettle on for the morning brew.

She took over making the tea and they settled into their pleasant morning routine. Sipping the tea, she smiled across at her boss and noticed that, although he was still very pale and looked extremely tired, he appeared a little less dishevelled than usual.

"Excellent tea, as usual, my dear." He paused and then continued: "I have a favour to ask of you, Lilian."

"Ask away, Mr. Robbins."

"I've decided I need to get away for a bit and the peace of the Scottish moors is calling to me. I feel if I can walk those hills again in solitude I might be able to find peace of mind again. So I wonder if you feel you could cope to keep the shop going by yourself?"

Lilian opened her mouth to impulsively agree but he went on – "Don't answer straight away, dear. Think about it and maybe you should speak to your parents about it."

At that moment the shop bell rang, announcing the day's first customer, so Lilian put down her cup went out to greet them. The morning was quite busy but while Lilian tidied and catalogued she considered Albert's proposal and increasingly came to the conclusion that she would be able to manage the shop and she did want to help him as much as she could. Possibly she would be called up for war work at some time in the future, but for now she felt she could manage the shop: after all, she had been doing practically everything for the last few weeks and months, and if it helped Albert, even better.

When they had their afternoon break Lilian immediately told Albert of her decision and clearly saw the relief spread across his face.

"That's a weight off my mind. Thank you, dear. You've already got the front door key so I just need to give you the safe key and show you about ordering."

The 'safe' was actually a small wall cabinet in the kitchen area, and Lilian knew all she needed to know about ordering but she didn't say anything.

At the end of the day, just as Lilian was leaving. Muriel jumped off the bus and ran along the road to meet her friend. The girls walked back together while Lilian told Muriel about taking over the shop.

"That'll be great experience for you," said Muriel, "and I'm sure you'll manage – you're really organised."

Lilian nodded and smiled, still a little unsure of what she was taking on.

"Anyway," Muriel went on, "tell me all about your date on Saturday – I'm dying to hear how you got on."

"Yes, I thought I'd see you at church yesterday, eager to hear all about it."

"Well, actually, I was otherwise engaged. I had a date with Jack; that's the chap I danced with at the Manor."

"I didn't know you were going to see him again."

"Neither did I because I left the party when I couldn't find you, but he asked around and found out where I live and turned up the other day."

"Oh, I'm so glad – I did feel guilty that you left early because of me. What's he like?"

"He's really rather nice. Not exactly the man of my dreams but he's fun to be with and that's the main thing. But never mind about me, tell me about Michael. I can see you're getting all dreamy just thinking about him."

"Mmm, I had a lovely time – we went for a long walk along the river in Market Stamford, then he took me for tea at the Stamford Grange Hotel! It was ever so smart and we chatted for ages."

"Wow! What did your mum say?"

"I didn't tell her, actually. I expect she thought you and I were shopping as usual."

"Don't you think your parents would approve, then? Goodness, you're old enough to have a boyfriend."

"The trouble is he's only a private and they might not like the way we met."

"Yuk! You mean you haven't been formally introduced," replied Muriel with more than a hint of sarcasm. She was itching to say more about people with snobbish attitudes but kept quiet to avoid hurting her friend. "Well, he sounds lovely to me and if you don't want to tell them yet, you can always say you're coming over to mine."

"Thanks, Muriel, I will tell them later on if I'm still seeing him. I know it's silly really."

The girls had arrived at the point where their paths diverged and stopping for a moment, Muriel saw a visitor going into Lilian's house.

"Looks like you've got a visitor," she commented, nodding up the road.

"That's Mr. Blackstock, remember I told you about him? Oh, I rather wish he wasn't there tonight – I want to check with my parents that they're happy for me to help Albert out."

"Does he usually stay long?"

"Yes, he's always going on about his investments and 'realising' his capital."

"Mmm, that sounds posh but mind you, I'm sure I've seen him coming out of old Mrs. Skinner's round the back of us – you know her that lets out rooms. And that's not posh!"

"No, it's not, is it? Bye, Muriel, see you soon."

"Bye, Lil, be good! And if you can't be good, be careful!" With a cheery wave off she ran, down towards home while Lilian dawdled a bit, thinking perhaps she'd just try to have a word with Agnes on the quiet.

In the end the two men went off down to the pub for a quick drink so Lilian was able to speak to her mother as they cleared away the tea things.

Agnes was very unsure to begin with and her first response was concern over Lilian's youth to be taking on such a responsibility.

"I'll have to speak to your father about it when he comes in."

"I know I can cope with it, Mother – the fact is I've been more or less running the shop for weeks now."

"We'll see what your father says, but it would be rather nice if you were in charge of the lending library."

At that moment Tom came running down the stairs to ask Lilian to give him a hand with the jigsaw he was starting and then they soon settled down with it at the kitchen table while Agnes went off to the parlour to carry on knitting comforters for the troops.

"I saw your sweetheart earlier," grinned Tom.

"He's not my sweetheart. Where did you see him?"

"Course he's your sweetheart, I saw him kissing you on Saturday. Anyway he's right nice – he were really friendly to me."

"Well, don't say anything O.K.? 'Cos he's just a friend."

"If you say so," said Tom, with a great big wink.

Before long, they heard the men come back from the pub and Blackstock still stayed on in the parlour. Lilian hoped her mother would wait until he'd gone to broach the subject of the shop but he was still there when she went up to bed so further discussion would have to wait until morning.

As in most households breakfast was always rushed, especially now with Tom to get off to school but Lilian's parents made time to tell her that they would be happy for her to take over the business on a temporary basis as long as there was a written agreement signed by Albert.

"You don't need a solicitor or anything but Desmond said he will gladly witness the contract."

"What did you have to tell him for?" grumbled Lilian.

"He's a man of the world and has lots of experience in business matters. Show some more respect my girl."

"Sorry, Father."

Knowing that was the end of the discussion, for Edward never wavered once he had made his decision, Lilian finished her toast and left for work.

At the corner she was delighted to see Michael waiting for her.

"Hello, what are you doing here?"

"Waiting for you. Got a couple of hours free so what better than to walk my girl to work?" So saying, he kissed her cheek and pulled her hand through his arm.

By mutual unspoken agreement they slowed their pace so that the short walk to work took as long as possible. Lilian told him all about the new situation with Albert and as she had hoped, he was very encouraging. All too soon they arrived at the shop and he stooped to kiss her goodbye, saying, "I often see that young lad of yours about, so if I can't get to see you, I can give him a message, can't I?"

"Of course, Tom's a good boy."

"O.K., then. Bye for now, my darling."

Lilian stood transfixed as he marched off. He had called her his darling! Gathering her thoughts and taking a deep breath, she rummaged in her bag for the keys.

As soon as she opened the door her elation of the past few minutes evaporated. The silence was palpable, she didn't call out as she usually would; somehow she knew there was no point.

In the little back kitchen two cups and saucers were laid out, biscuits were on a plate and the kettle was still warm, but she knew the house was empty. With her heart in her mouth she started up the stairs, calling out this time for she wouldn't dream of entering Albert's private rooms without announcing herself.

"Are you there, Mr. Robbins? Are you alright?"

There was no reply and the sitting room was empty, though neat and tidy. She looked around to see if there was any message before peeping into the bedroom where she found the bed had been stripped and left prepared in a military manner. She rushed downstairs to the back door: perhaps he had just popped outside but clearly he hadn't as she had to unbolt the door.

He had just gone with no message and no farewell.

Chapter 8

Few of the customers and borrowers were surprised at Lilian taking on the shop because most had realised that Albert had been finding it increasingly difficult to maintain his outward appearance of stability. They readily accepted Lilian's explanation that he was taking a few weeks out to rest and visit old friends.

There had been some consternation at home when she told them of his simply having disappeared; clearly there was now no written agreement and without a forwarding address, the only option seemed to be to carry on in the hope that Albert would make contact in due course. If Lilian didn't keep the shop and library running, the community would lose a valuable resource and she would be out of a job and in that case would probably need to join the Land Army or some other designated war work.

At the shop she managed very well, maintaining everything in the highly professional way she had learned from Albert. Each week she paid the cash into the bank and paid herself exactly the same wages she had always had. All these transactions were faithfully recorded in a special notebook kept under the counter.

cuits*

The notebook was one she had coveted for some time, being of beautiful quality and decorated with a delightful pattern of dragonflies winging across a pond; she put the cost price for the book into the till, telling herself it wasn't too extravagant because this was very important and every time she made an entry the mere sight and feel of the notebook gave her pleasure.

At first, the extra responsibility and slightly longer hours meant Lilian felt more tired at the end of the day, but she was careful to hide this from her parents in case they stopped her doing it. Overall she was really enjoying the feeling of coping with the challenge of taking on sole management and so far she hadn't had one rude or dissatisfied customer.

Most days Muriel popped in on her way to or from work, as she was on shift work now, to have a quick chat and provide moral support. Lilian usually welcomed her friend's visits as it could get very quiet sometimes, usually before lunch and around teatime. Even though she could always occupy herself with a good book, the silence in the shop was oppressive and she really missed Albert's genial presence. One day she mentioned this to Muriel who, as usual, had a ready answer.

"What you should do is switch on the wireless and listen to 'Music While You Work'. We have it on in the factory all the time and it's ever so good; we all sing along with the tunes – really cheers you up."

"There's no wireless down here – Albert's is up in the sitting room."

"Well, bring it down, then!"

"No, I don't think I'd better do that."

"O.K., just a suggestion."

When Muriel had gone, Lilian considered the idea and thought perhaps she could try turning the wireless on quite loud and leaving the door open.

"Yes," she thought, "I'll try that tomorrow."

It did work pretty well; in the quiet periods the background music just kept the feeling of loneliness away. What it didn't keep away was the ever-f1present anxiety that she had had no word from Michael since the day he had met her on the way to work. She had seen him once a few days ago when a huge Army truck had thundered down the road and there he was standing in the back holding onto a rail and waving to her frantically.

She stood quite still, although she felt like breaking into a run, and waved and waved and waved until the truck was out of sight. She wondered how it was possible to miss someone so much when in truth they hadn't really spent that much time together. Thinking back over the time they had spent together was her favourite daydream which always made her smile and say a little prayer for their future.

It was at just such a moment that Tom burst in the shop door with a huge grin on his face.

"Hello, Tom," she smiled, "have you come to borrow a book."

"Oh, no thanks – I've got a book – I've come with a message," he replied with a wide-eyed look of mystery.

"From Mother?" queried Lilian, not daring to think it was from her beau.

"Nope." He grinned even wider and pulling a folded envelope out of his pocket, proceeded to hide it behind his back.

"Give it here, you little monster," laughed Lilian, almost sure it must be from Michael and really impatient to find out.

He continued to tease her by holding the envelope out of reach and then pretending to kiss it. As she grabbed it he let go but didn't wait to see her read it, saying, "Phwar, I'm out of here, I bet it's really soppy. Bye, Lil, see you at home."

"Thanks, Tom, bye, bye."

Thank goodness the shop was empty so she could sink down into her favourite chair at the back of the shelves to open the longed-for message.

My Dearest Lilian,

I'm hoping that I can catch young Tom to carry this message to you. He is seen quite often with a few of his friends up around the Manor.

The work in our section has been very strenuous of late – really heavy training – very erratic – that's why I haven't been able to see you. I am sorry. I hope you understand.

I think about you every day and can't wait to see you again and maybe we can go out for tea again and perhaps the flicks as well. I don't know what kind of films you like – just one more thing I'm longing to learn about you.

Have to close now, my love, think about me when you can.

Michael XX

It was far more thrilling than she had dared to imagine – sweet and loving and forward-looking. Lilian took a deep breath, smiling and feeling a happy, hugging-herself sensation. She read the letter twice over before holding it close to her heart and folding it carefully to keep safe. As it was nearly closing time she neatly slipped the missive into her bag before beginning the cashing up routine and checking that all was secure for the night.

On the way home she went over the message in her mind again and began to plan her reply. She wanted it to be loving and thoughtful but not too gushing – quite a difficult compromise. Of course Muriel would have lots of advice but this was something she would keep entirely to herself – it was too precious at the moment to share.

After supper Lilian and Tom played dominoes in the kitchen while her parents followed the nightly ritual of listening to the news on the radio. Agnes made a pot of tea to take through to the parlour after pouring a cup for each of the youngsters. She was halfway out of the door carrying the tray when Tom reached for a biscuit.

"Don't dunk your biscuit, Tom. I've told you we don't do that in this house – it's common."

Looking a picture of innocence, the lad bit into the Lincoln cream but proceeded to dunk it as soon as she was gone, whispering under his breath: "Never mind, I am common."

"Thanks for bringing the letter, Tom," Lilian began.

The lad looked up and grinned: "S'alright."

"Would you be able to take a reply, do you think?"

Tom nodded, slammed down the last domino to take the game and leaned back, looking very pleased with himself.

"I knew he was your sweetheart!"

"Shh," whispered Lilian, "can you keep it secret?"

"Course I can. Mind you, I've already told me mates!"

Lilian tutted and ruffled his hair fondly. "Just one more game then I'll go and write the letter. I'll put it under your door. O.K.?"

"Sure. My lips are sealed. I can take it after school tomorrow."

It didn't take her as long as she'd thought to compose the letter and when it was finished she felt it struck just the right note. She had used paper and envelope from a lovely stationery set that had been one of her Christmas gifts last year; the paper was smooth, slightly creamy in colour, and inside the flap of each envelope was a prettily drawn lily. She had liked the attention to detail before and now thought maybe Michael would find it romantic.

Just before closing time next day Tom again came into the shop to Lilian's surprise; she hadn't expected a reply so soon. But the letter he pulled out of his pocket, along with some string and an acorn, was the one she had written. Her momentary elation was dashed as Tom handed her the letter, saying, "Sorry, Lil, I couldn't give it to him. I waited a long time without seeing anyone so I asked the sentry and he said they've all gone."

"Gone? Do you mean for good?"

"Dunno." He shook his head and shrugged, looking nearly as disappointed as Lilian.

At that moment the door opened again, the shop bell clanging and a breathless customer came in – a young woman Lilian had never seen before.

"Oh! I'm so glad you're still open, I thought I might have missed you," she began.

Snapping back into business mode, Lilian smiled and replied, "I was about to close but how can I help you?"

"I need some of that special lightweight writing paper. My fellow's going overseas and I must use that so I can write to him every day!"

Registering the ironic coincidence of the girl's request, Lilian directed her to the airmail paper and nodded with a little wry smile to Tom as he left the shop. When the short transaction was completed she locked the shop door and followed the routine of closing up. Finally she picked up the redundant letter, rather crumpled by now, and put it in her bag before beginning the walk home.

As she walked an idea came to her – maybe Muriel had seen her boyfriend Jack who was in the same outfit as Michael – maybe she knew something about their disappearance. So, instead of going straight home she went to Muriel's house and knocked on the door.

Muriel's mother came to the door, wiping her hands on her apron and smiled as soon as she saw Lilian.

"Hello, dear, I'm afraid Muriel's not here at the moment; she's on a late shift today. I'll tell her you called to see her, shall I?"

"Oh, yes. Thank you. Sorry to have bothered you," said Lilian, turning away and walking back down the lane.

At home Agnes was in a rush, bustling around because she needed to get to the first aid course that was being held in the church hall.

Lilian was glad of the distraction because she knew she wasn't the world's best actress and not good at hiding her feelings.

"You go to the meeting, Mother." she said, "I'll clear up here."

"Aren't you coming to the class, dear?"

"No, not today, I'm a bit tired, I'll come next week."

"Very well, Lilian. Thank you, dear. See you later."

Next morning Muriel popped into the shop on her way to her shift.

"Hello, Lil. Mum said you called round yesterday and you seemed a bit upset. Is anything wrong?"

"I'm not sure, Muriel. Did you know all the soldiers from the Manor have left?"

"Have they? How d'ya know?"

"Tom found out. He went to take a letter to Michael and the sentry told him."

"A letter to Michael – mmm – who would that be from, I wonder?"

Lilian just blushed but said nothing.

"I haven't seen Jack for a few days either but I'spect they'll be back before long."

"Do you think so?" asked Lilian, feeling a little bit hopeful.

"Oh sure – it'll just be some exercise, I reckon. My dad says they're always doing exercises and not much else."

"I hope you're right. I wish I'd seen him to say goodbye."

"You're really stuck on him, aren't you? No need to answer – I know you well enough, Lilian Woodridge."

This brought a smile to Lilian's face.

"Listen, I've got to run or I'm gonna be late back. Why don't we go to the Curzon on Saturday – they've got the new Laurel and Hardy film on – that'll cheer you up."

"O.K. That would be nice."

"Fine, meet you at the cinema around six. Bye now!"

So saying, Muriel flew out of the door, almost knocking the postman over. He was delivering three letters – two invoices from suppliers and one with a postmark from Scotland.

Hooray, Albert has written.

It was a lovely positive letter, starting with an apology that he'd left without saying goodbye but explaining that he felt he just had to get away and hoped he had not upset her.

The letter went on to describe how the peace of the countryside where he was staying had such a calming and restorative effect on him.

Finally he asked Lilian to send him a bank statement and any outstanding bills so that he could send cheques to cover them and at least take the admin burden from her. Although there seemed to be no definite plan to return, it was certainly implied that he'd be back.

Lilian was so relieved firstly to hear that he was alright and seemed to be recovering, and secondly, that she would be able to show the letter to her parents because Desmond Blackstock had been making noises about helping her with the financial side of the business and she certainly didn't want that.

The following days were really quite busy in the shop/library; it seemed that many in the village suddenly developed a need for stationery or something to read. Quite a few of the village also just popped in for a chat, which was really nice.

Towards lunchtime Lilian was behind the counter parcelling up a couple of items she had promised to deliver to old Mrs. Prendergust when the door opened: looking up, the scissors dropped out of her hand and she gasped.

It was HIM!

Chapter 9

Like an automaton Lilian moved round the counter and into the shop, at first expressionless but then with the widest of smiles: "Michael."

"Lilian."

"You're back!"

"I came as soon as I could."

In the next moment, and almost without knowing how it happened, they were in each other's arms and he held her tight – so tight. Lilian moved her head and Michael found her lips with his: a kiss at first, tender, but soon deepening into a yearning and passion that neither had known before.

Moving slightly away to catch her breath, Lilian turned to the door, putting the Closed sign on and locking it. Hand in hand she led him to the two comfy chairs of the little library and they sat, never taking their eyes off each other.

For the next hour or so they talked and kissed and talked some more, making up for lost time together. Lilian was vaguely aware that she should have gone home for some lunch after locking up but it just seemed that the only place she belonged was here with her love.

At last Michael looked at his watch and said, "I must be going, my dear, but can I see you again tomorrow?"

"Yes, of course."

"I'll call for you here after closing – is that alright?"

Lilian just nodded and walked with him to the door where they parted with a kiss and a gentle wave. The rest of the afternoon passed in something of a blur for Lilian. Customers came and went; presumably she served them correctly but she was walking on air in a golden daze.

It wasn't until she was walking home that it occurred to Lilian that her mother would wonder why she hadn't come home for lunch. She could hardly admit she'd had a delightful tryst with a young man – what reason could she give? Unused to any type of subterfuge, she was really at a loss – maybe an awkward customer? Still undecided, she arrived home and went straight into the kitchen. Tom was there eating a doorstep of bread with a smear of treacle.

"Hello, Lil, yer mum's out – another meeting!"

"Was she worried when I didn't come home for lunch?"

"No, it's O.K. I saw yer fella down the lane so I covered for you. I said there was a delivery van at the shop."

"Oh, thanks, Tom. What would I do without you? I suppose this is going to cost me next week's sweet ration?"

"Yup!"

Over the next two or three weeks Lilian and Michael met almost every day, even if only for a few minutes when he could get away. Their feelings for each other rapidly grew stronger and Lilian at any rate lived for the moments they were together. Far from wanting to keep their romance a secret she now found herself wanting to shout it from the rooftops.

Thus she instigated a confidential heart-to-heart with Agnes one evening when they were alone in the kitchen clearing up after tea. "I'm popping out later, Mother. I've become friendly with a nice young man I met at the Manor social."

"That's nice, dear. Is he an officer?"

"No, but he's really nice and actually he would have gone to college if the war hadn't started."

"Where does he come from?"

"Down South, quite near London, I think, so he can't get home much and I wondered if he could ask him to tea on Sunday."

"I can see you're quite fond of him and you've certainly been quite bright-eyed these last few weeks."

Lilian blushed and smiled, waiting for her mother's decision.

"I'm sure it will be fine for him to come to tea. I can make some fish paste sandwiches and scones with home-made jam. I expect he'd like that. Of course not so long ago, I would have done vol-au-vents and sausage rolls, maybe even éclairs but never mind, times have changed and we must get on with it."

"Thank you, Mother," said Lilian as she hugged Agnes and smiled at how proud she and her father were that her mother had really come out of her shell and become a stalwart of the village war effort.

Lilian couldn't wait to invite Michael to tea so it was almost the first thing she said to him that evening after greeting each other with a gentle kiss. His reaction was a little disappointing: he didn't refuse but he didn't seem that keen either, and when he said he thought he'd be on duty on Sunday it seemed like an excuse.

Undaunted, Lilian replied, "Well, perhaps in a couple of weeks, then."

"Yes, that'd be nice."

Then the subject was changed and the rest of the evening went well.

His reluctance still disturbed Lilian, however, and she was glad on Sunday after church to have a chance for a long heart-to-heart with Muriel. It was the first time the girls had spent so much time together for ages, what with Lilian busy in the shop or out with Michael and Muriel on quite irregular shifts.

Cheerful as ever, Muriel laughed off her friend's concerns:

"Ooh and he hasn't even met your mum yet!"

"What do you mean?"

"Just joking, Lil. Everyone in the village really respects your mum and the way she's buckled down and organised all the blackout curtains and the evacuees and goodness knows what else. No, the thing is with fellas, they kind of get cold feet if they think you're getting too serious – that's all, I expect."

"Don't you think I should ask him, then?"

"Yes, you can but tell you what, let's suggest we go out as a foursome sometime, you and Michael, me and Jack – that'll be fun and it's sort of more casual."

Eventually, actually more than a month later, the Sunday tea did happen. Michael arrived on the doorstep clutching a tiny bunch of violets for Agnes, which delighted her. After introductions and a few minutes' small talk, Lilian and her mother left the men alone while they finished preparing the tea.

"I can see why you like him, dear," said Agnes as soon as the kitchen door was closed. "He's very nice-looking and he has such lovely manners. The violets are a perfect gift."

Privately Lilian wondered why she'd never had any violets, but nevertheless was delighted by her mother's positive first impression.

Teatime was really pleasant – they chatted about all sorts of topics and the sandwiches, some egg, some fish paste, were delicious. Michael enthused about the lightness of the scones, which pleased Agnes no end.

"Is young Tom not coming for his tea?" Michael asked.

"Oh, you've met him, have you?" Agnes replied.

"Yes, I've seen him around a few times, he seems a really nice lad."

"He's settled in really well and don't you worry, I've kept some back for him. Can't have him wasting away."

"No chance of that," said Edward. "He's a different lad from the scrawny little runt who came here. The good country air and Agnes' cooking have put roses in his cheeks alright."

When everyone was sufficed, Edward at the head of the table asked, "Have you young people some plans for the evening?"

Lilian replied, "I think we're meeting Muriel and Jack at the pub for a game of shove ha'penny later."

Michael took up the story, saying, "Yes, we've been out in a foursome with them a few times. Jack is a very nice chap and

Muriel's, well what would you say? – a caution?"

"I know what you mean," smiled Agnes as she began to clear away the tea things. Lilian rose to give a hand.

"No, off you go, you two have a lovely evening."

Goodbyes and thank yous were exchanged at the door and Michael held Lilian's hand as they walked off down the lane. Before they reached the turning to Muriel's house Michael stopped and pulled her towards him.

"Let's not meet the others," he said.

"Why?"

"I want you all to myself," he replied.

"We can't do that," began Lilian as he held her close and kissed her with a passion and longing as never before.

They only broke away when they heard a long, low wolf whistle.

Of course it was Tom in the hedge nearby.

"Go away, you little monster!" cried Lilian.

"Sorry, Lil, sorry, sir." He darted off and they couldn't be cross with his cheeky smile.

"You're really fond of him, aren't you, darling?" said Michael.

"Yes, he's like the brother I never had."

"Don't get too close to him, though. Remember when the war's over he'll go back to the city."

Chapter 10

With scant regard for the joys of young love, the War Office and 'powers that be' decided Michael was to go away again. This time the duration was to be about three or four weeks to help with training on some new equipment. At least this time they had some warning and, although the destination was unknown, it wasn't a deep secret like before. He gently explained as much as he could while they strolled hand-in-hand along the back lanes between the shop and Lilian's home – whenever he could, Michael tried to walk her home after work.

"Will you miss me when I'm away?" he asked provocatively, knowing full well what the answer would be.

"Of course I will but I shan't mind so much now that I know why you're going and that it's not for too long." Lilian let go of his hand and put her arm through his to draw a little closer. "Just think, my love, if there hadn't been a war we wouldn't have met. I know it's awful in lots of ways but it's been good for us, hasn't it?"

"Mmm, we've got a lot to be thankful for. Make sure you remember that when I'm away. Don't go dating any other soldiers, will you?!"

"As if I would – I'm going to be too busy anyway, what with the shop and helping mother at home and with her war work; she's organising a social now for the village and evacuees' parents – it'll be lots of work."

"She's a real brick, your mum, different to what she seems at first."

In spite of what she had said, Lilian couldn't help a few tears when Michael called in to say goodbye a few days later. Wiping the tears away, he lifted her hand to his lips and said, "We'll soon be together again."

With the blind confidence of youth neither of them foresaw any way that they could be parted in the long term.

***

The social-cum-party for the evacuees and their host families had been Agnes' idea a couple of weeks ago after she, one evening, came upon Tom looking really glum while puzzling over one of his schoolbooks at the kitchen table. Thinking he was needing some help with his studies, she asked what the trouble was and when he looked up was surprised to see his face red and grubby as though he had just wiped away tears. The lad was generally feisty enough to tough out any school problems so she tried to coax his problems out of him over one of their regular games of dominoes. Eventually he discovered that it was the day of his mother's birthday and it had received his feelings of homesickness.

"Do you have special celebrations when it's her birthday?"

"No, not really," replied Tom. "Usually me gran brings round a lardy cake or summat and we sing Happy Birthday – That's all. But I'm really sorry I didn't see her this year – she's me mum after all."

The lad's bottom lip quivered and he swallowed hard, clearly fighting to maintain his tough exterior.

Agnes was touched by the lad's thoughtfulness and concern for his mother, especially as since the first night when he apparently had a nightmare he had been no trouble at all. She knew some of the evacuees in the village had been, or still were, desperately homesick.

Casting around for a way to help, Agnes came up with an idea: "Tell you what, Tom, I've got a few pretty cards in my drawer upstairs. I keep them in case I forget someone's birthday. You can write a nice message and we'll send it to your mother straight away. She won't mind it being a day or so late."

"Oh, thank you, Mrs. Woodridge. She'd love that – she don't usually get a card."

After Tom had written the card and rushed down to the postbox to send it, his carefree mood was fully restored and he was hungry again.

When he was in bed, Agnes decided to run her idea for a social gathering past Edward to get his opinion. Edward's first response was predictably concern that his wife was giving herself more work and more problems but when she explained about Tom he began to appreciate her reasons.

"How's it going to be paid for, though, Agnes?! Parties cost money."

"Well, the church hall will be free, cups of tea don't cost much and I'm sure all the families will be happy to bring a plate of sandwiches or a jelly like we do for the Christmas party."

Edward could see his wife's newfound determined wartime spirit was not going to be thwarted, so he gave in, knowing he, too, would probably be roped in to help.

The very next day Agnes began to visit all the host families to explain her plan and gauge their opinions. Almost without exception the families thought it a good idea and soon a date was set and some of Agnes' famous lists were being drawn up: helpers to set up, helpers to make tea, helpers to clear away, and promises of who'd bring what.

Lilian helped her mother send out the invitations to all the parents or guardians of the children and it was decided not to say too much to the children in case for some reason their parent couldn't come.

***

Before they knew it, the day of the party was imminent; it was to be on a Sunday afternoon so that as many guests as possible would be available. Almost everyone in the village, even those not involved with evacuees, lent a hand in some way. Much to Lilian's surprise, Desmond Blackstock volunteered to help on the day and set to with a will setting up trestle tables and putting up chairs.

Muriel and her mum were helping Lilian and one other lady to collect and lay out the food as well as boil the kettles for tea. The spread looked really festive, for there was an amazing variety, all laid out on different but charmingly patterned plates: there were egg sandwiches, paste sandwiches, cheese and pickle, sausage rolls and mince pies (mincemeat left over from Christmas) as well as fairy cakes and jellies of every colour. The lads of Tom's little gang were hungrily eyeing the feast until Muriel called out, "You kids! Keep your thieving mitts off the grub – you've gotta wait till teatime. Go and amuse yourselves till then."

They good-naturedly wandered off to the far side of the hall where Blackstock had set up an area for some party games.

Muriel nudged Lilian and whispered, "Look at that, your Mr. Blackstock's doing games for the kids!"

"He's not my Mr. Blackstock but I'm amazed. Mother will be pleased."

Just at that moment outside the post office the local bus was pulling up and disgorging an excited group of visitors. The conductor pointed the way to the church hall and they almost ran towards it, most laden down with shopping bags of whatever they could get hold of as a treat or gift.

One of the younger girls was the first to catch sight of her auntie and then her mum, taking a few seconds to register their presence before running the full length of the hall and excitedly greeting them. The other children saw this happening and a number of other adults arriving, so they began to huddle at the door hoping to see their parents arrive and few were disappointed. Tom hung back, staying out of the fray and trying to look very nonchalant, not really expecting that his mother would be one of the group.

But there she was! The youngest prettiest of all the mums, at least in his opinion, stood in the doorway and looked around before catching sight of her boy and waving. All the nonchalance thrown aside, Tom flew down the hall and into a rare and lovely hug.

"Cor, Mum, I didn't know you was comin'."

"Well, I had to change me shifts but I thought I couldn't miss seeing you and finding out how you're goin' on." "Well, it's not bad really, only the place all round is so quiet."

"Nothing wrong with quiet, it's better than – well, never mind. I brought you some lardy cake and a pair of football boots that your cousin has grown out of!"

"Thanks, Mum. Shall I get you a cuppa tea?"

Agnes had been watching the reunions at a distance really to make sure that none of the children became upset if their family didn't arrive. Luckily that wasn't the case – everyone had someone to visit. That was such a relief as that had been the main concern voiced by the host families. Most pleasing of all was the little show of affection between Tom and his mum.

Seeing that Tom had gone to fetch a cup of tea, Agnes made her way over to the young woman.

"Hello, you must be Tom's mum. I'm Mrs. Woodridge – Tom's staying with us."

She extended her hand and Betty Brown shook it with a surprisingly firm grip.

"Pleased ter meet you – I 'ope e's behaving himself."

"Yes he's being a good boy, aren't you, Tom?"

Being talked about in this way deeply embarrassed Tom so he put down the tea and shuffled uncomfortably. Agnes couldn't help noticing the bright red nail polish that the young woman was wearing with matching lipstick and that her blonde hair, dressed in a modern coiled style, was showing unmistakenly dark roots.

Struggling not to show her disapproval, she stayed chatting for a few minutes longer before making an excuse to check in the kitchen.

The girls had been peering through the kitchen hatch enjoying the happy little reunions in the hall and Muriel had very soon noticed Betty Brown.

"Wow, young Tom's mum has come dressed to the nines. She looks a bit of a goer. I like her dress: I wonder where she got that."

"Not in Market Stanford, that's for sure."

"Ooops, your mum's coming over – better get back to work."

Hesitating a moment longer, though, Muriel nudged her friend and said, "Look at that, someone else likes the look of her." Desmond Blackstock had marched straight up to Mrs. Brown, extended his hand and half-bowed in a very gracious manner. He then proceeded to engage her in conversation for most of the afternoon.

All too soon the party came to an end; many cups of tea had been consumed and all the plates and dishes were empty; a few tearful farewells but all in all the event had been a great success. Now that it was all over Agnes suddenly flagged and was really glad when Edward took over by asking Desmond to organise the volunteers while he escorted his wife home to rest. On the way out they checked with Lilian and Muriel that the kitchen helpers were in place and Edward whispered to Lilian, "Just taking Mother home to rest – she's all in. Will you take the keys over to the vicarage when you leave?"

Tom and a couple of his mates helped as well and soon the whole area was spick and span.

As the final group of helpers left, Lilian and Muriel met Blackstock at the entrance and he made a comment about how successful the afternoon had been.

"Yes," replied Lilian, "Mother will be really pleased. Thank you very much for all your help, Mr. Blackstock."

"It was a pleasure, my dear. Please tell your father I'll be in the pub if he'd like to join me."

The social was the talk of the village for a few days, everyone feeling that it had been a good thing for the children and the families. Agnes knew she had overstretched herself a bit and wisely slowed down for a time, taking a bit of a rest each afternoon.

Each Friday it was part of Lilian's routine to take the week's takings to the bank for paying in; she usually chose mid-afternoon because this was the quietest time both in the bank and the shop, but today there was quite a queue for the cashier. As the queue moved forward it was Desmond Blackstock who walked back from the counter and he stopped to greet her most charmingly. He asked after her mother, they chatted about the weather and then he surprised Lilian by inviting her for a cup of tea. Her first impulse was to refuse but remembering how helpful he had been at the party she thought it would be churlish to refuse.

"That's very kind of you, Mr. Blackstock, but I can't stay long because I've got to get back to the shop."

"That's quite alright. I quite understand."

As soon as Lilian's banking was done he took her arm and they left to cross the road to the tea shop.

He was looking very pleased with himself.

Chapter 11

Lilian and Blackstock conversed amiably over a pot of tea; he could be pleasant and very entertaining when he wanted. She found she rather liked the Irish lilt in his voice and the wistful note as he talked about his home in Ireland. When she asked about his plans to return to his homeland he just laughed and changed the subject.

As they were finishing their tea Desmond suddenly asked after Michael (apparently he had seen them together) and his comments were vaguely lascivious in a rather unpleasant way. Not wanting to be rude but unwilling to speak about Michael to him, Lilian jumped up and said she must be getting back to the shop, which was true.

Unlocking the front door and going into the shop, she found herself shuddering and quite upset at the insinuations he had made – it was almost as though he had somehow sullied her precious relationship with Michael. She took off her jacket, turned the shop sign to OPEN and reached into her bag where she still had a small bunch of wood anemones that she had collected on a walk with her beau and pressed. They were becoming a bit battered, as was her resolution to remain positive.

Without the distraction of organising the social, Lilian had begun to miss Michael a good deal and it was now long past the time he had expected to be back. She couldn't help worrying and with this last verbal abuse she could no longer hold back the tears.

She was still sniffing a bit when the shop bell rang, announcing a customer; every time the door opened she hoped and prayed it would be Michael but it was the vicar's wife, Mrs. Martin, this time.

"Are you alright, dear?" she asked, seeing the girl red-eyed.

"Oh, yes – it's a bit of a cold, I think," replied Lilian. "How can I help?"

Mrs. Martin wasn't convinced but didn't pursue the matter. The rest of the afternoon was busier than usual so Lilian had no more time to reflect on her worries. Her melancholy feeling didn't return until she was walking home along the paths she and Michael had often strolled along hand in hand; to cheer herself up she took the turning to Muriel's house instead of going straight home, hoping that her friend would be at home. One of Muriel's younger brothers answered the door with a friendly grin and immediately turned to holler, "Mu, it's for you!" making it like a little song and already cheering Lilian with his cheeky manner.

Muriel came straight away from the kitchen, wiping her hands on a tea towel, and drew her friend into the cheerful chaos that was their living room.

"How do you do it, Lilian Woodridge? You must have known the kettle has just boiled. Come and help me brew the tea and then we can have a nice chat."

They sat at the kitchen table with a cup of tea and a piece of flapjack that Muriel's mum had made.

"Come on now, tell your Auntie Muriel – what's the matter? You look as if you've lost a quid and found five bob."

"Nothing's the matter. I just wondered if you'd heard from Jack at all, only Michael thought he'd be back by now and I haven't heard a thing."

"No, I haven't heard anything and you know what they say – no news is good news."

"I suppose so – it's just that I thought they'd be back by now and I can't help worrying."

Muriel took a sip of tea and shook her head. "What you need is something to take your mind off things and I have an idea. Let's go dancing at the weekend, there's a regular do on Saturdays at the town hall in Market Stamford. Gloria says it's quite good."

"We-ell," replied Lilian uncertainly before adding, "Why not? – it sounds like fun."

They drank their tea and chatted a bit longer before Lilian got up to leave, feeling much more cheerful.

"You've cheered me up as usual, Muriel."

"Always glad to be of service." Her friend grinned.

At home after supper, Lilian picked up her knitting to carry on with the pretty lacy jumper she was making to try to finish it so she could wear it to the dance.

The days in the shop were sometimes a bit lonely now: although Albert had never been much of a talker, he was company on the quiet days. She did her best to keep busy and looked up expectantly each time the shop bell rang – hoping to see Michael's handsome face. Each time it was someone else her disappointment increased.

A few evenings later, still working away at the knitting by the kitchen table, the back door suddenly flew open and Tom dashed in with a big grin on his face.

"What have you been up to, young man?"

"Nutthin! You'll find out. Can I have a drink?"

"There's some tea in the pot, help yourself."

Next thing she heard was the front door knocker.

"I wonder who that could be at this time," she said, putting down her knitting and going to answer it.

Michael was standing on the porch looking weary but incredibly handsome.

Lilian couldn't believe her eyes and for a moment neither spoke. Pulling off his cap, Michael smiled cautiously and said, "I hope you don't mind me calling – we just got back and I couldn't wait to see you."

With her heart pounding joyfully she reached towards him, saying, "Of course I don't mind – come on in – you look as though you need a cup of tea."

Once inside the hall he took her in his arms and whispered, "I need a kiss first."

After more than one kiss they made it to the kitchen where Tom was munching an apple and grinning all over his face. To this he added a huge wink and informed them he was going up to do his homework, which was patently untrue because he rarely bothered with such things.

Michael sat at the kitchen table while Lilian made a pot of tea and a slice of cheese on toast. The homely activity felt warm in every sense.

He gratefully demolished the little repast and they chatted, holding hands for a while until he said, "I'm afraid I can't stay long as I'm due back for a 'debrief' but then I should get some time off after that, so we can be together for a while."

"That'll be lovely," whispered Lilian. "I've missed you so much."

"Me, too," he murmured taking her into his arms as if she were his most precious possession.

***

The plan for Sunday was to spend the whole day together so Lilian packed up a simple picnic of cheese and pickle sandwiches, currant cake and a flask of tea, ignoring her mother's disapproval at missing church.

"It's just one week, Mother, and Michael may not have a free day again for ages."

They caught a bus to the next village and walked hand in hand around the charming village green with its duck pond and stone memorial of the Great War.

"What a lovely spot," Michael remarked. "Are we picnicking here?"

"We could, but I know a nicer place just a short walk away. We used to go there when I was a child, with my grandparents."

"O.K., whatever you say, my love."

The walk took them along a bridle path behind the churchyard and across a meadow to some woodland and finally a clearing where the land fell away to give a beautiful view over the rolling English countryside. There wasn't a house in sight and there wasn't a sound.

Lilian spread the travel rug she had carried and they sat side by side, drinking in the peace and beauty of the scene. Michael rested his elbows on his knees and mused: "This is what we're all fighting for, isn't it!? The peace and beauty of the countryside and the freedom to enjoy it with your girl beside you."

Turning to look at Lilian he added, "Your beautiful sweet girl," as he reached up to touch her cheek and push back a strand of hair.

She melted inside – his thoughts and ideas were always so close to thoughts of her own but he seemed to have the knack of putting them into words. No words were spoken for some minutes after that as they lay back together in a warm embrace to kiss gently.

Within moments the kisses were no longer gentle; they simultaneously pulled each other ever closer and the passion of their feelings rose to a pitch neither had ever felt before. As they broke away, Lilian straightened her skirt and leaned over to unpack the picnic.

They enjoyed the simple but deliciously fresh fare, both having healthy young appetites. They chatted in the relaxed way that lovers do, about their backgrounds, their lives, their hopes and dreams. While they talked Michael was winding and plaiting a few strands of grass; at first he seemed to be simply playing with the grass quite casually, but then he stopped talking to concentrate on the little project.

Lilian smiled and asked, "What are you making?"

"I'm making," he paused and held it up, "a ring for your finger. Darling Lilian, will you marry me?"

"Oh that's so romantic – yes, I will," she gasped.

He slipped the little ring of grass onto her finger and they kissed, clinging together as though they would never part.

This time they could not rein in their passion for each other.

The afternoon flew by in a haze of love – there was no past and no future only now. All too soon it was time to pack up and rush back to the village green to catch the bus. They almost ran most of the way hand in hand, as exhilarated and carefree as children.

On the way home Michael broached the subject of his need to speak with Edward about marrying her.

"Do you think he'll be available this evening?"

"Well, he usually goes down to the pub with his friends on a Sunday, so maybe one day in the week would be better."

"Fine, just let me know, my darling, I can't wait to tell the world you're going to be my wife."

***

He arrived bang on time in uniform looking so smart and handsome that Lilian caught her breath as she opened the front door. To her surprise he was looking really nervous, however, and he just paused for a moment to squeeze her hand before being shown into the parlour.

"I'll wait in the kitchen," murmured Lilian, to which Michael's response was just a nod as he closed the door looking like a man condemned!

Lilian put the kettle on, expecting that they'd have some tea and biscuits to celebrate their engagement. She hadn't shown anyone her precious little ring of grass, had just removed it gently and put it to press in her favourite book – a leather-bound copy of *Jane Eyre* which had been a school prize for storywriting. No diamond engagement ring could be more meaningful.

The pot of tea was brewing when she heard the door open and Michael came through to the kitchen. His face was a mask, showing no emotion whatsoever.

"Let's go for a walk, Lilian," he said as he almost pushed past her and out of the back door. She almost ran after him to catch up before linking her arm in his while wondering at his response.

"What did he say?"

The young man pursed his lips to a thin line and spat out, "Out of the question!"

"What do you mean?" Lilian was panting now, try to keep up with him and her throat was dry. "Stop, stop; tell me!" she begged.

They stopped and Michael took a deep breath before counting off on his fingers:

"You're too young; they don't know anything about me; and THERE'S A WAR ON!! He just wouldn't listen!"

Chapter 12

Lilian was left standing in the lane as he marched off at top speed to try to work out his anger, not wanting to upset his sweet girl by his own black mood. Her own disappointment and anger bubbled up inside like a boiling cauldron about to blow its top. By the time she'd run back to the house, though, she was sobbing and knew she was unable to confront her father, which had been her first thought. Instead she ran up to her room and nearly took the door off its hinges with an almighty slam.

In the parlour her parents looked up and Agnes went to put down her knitting.

"I'll go up and see if she's alright, shall I?"

"No, leave her, dear. There's nothing to say. There's no question of her marrying that young man. I just will not allow it." A generally mild-mannered man, Edward was fierce in what he saw as the protection of his daughter.

In her room Lilian threw herself on her bed sobbing uncontrollably, her feelings and her mind in a whirl, unable to take in the see-saw of emotions from elation to misery in such a short time.

It was dark when she awoke with an awful headache and damp pillow; rolling over, she got up to change into her nightdress and retrieve her little grass ring from the book. Her fury had worked itself out but she was left with a deep sadness underlining a quiet determination.

The disturbed and emotional night meant that Lilian was a bit late down for breakfast; in spite of holding a cold flannel to her eyes, they were still red. Agnes put a cup of tea down in front of her and began to make a piece of toast. Neither spoke until Lilian had eaten the toast with home-made marmalade.

Edward had already gone to work so mother and daughter were able to talk openly.

"I'll make a sandwich and have my lunch at the shop today." She rose and reached for the loaf.

"You can't avoid your father for ever, and in any case we've been perfectly reasonable. We haven't said you can't see him."

"You don't understand – I love him and he loves me – we just want to be together!"

"Lilian, you haven't known him very long – you just seem to be rushing headlong into this."

"I'm not! I'm not!" and the tears of frustration welled in her eyes again.

Agnes was unmoved, just continuing, "If he really cares for you, he'll wait until after the war or when you're twenty-one."

"You don't understand," Lilian repeated and gathered up her things to leave for work without a goodbye.

By the time she got to the shop she was late in opening up and there was a rather disgruntled customer waiting, who grumbled and tutted a bit while choosing a birthday card and a postcard. After that, though, the rest of the morning was really quiet and Lilian fell to ruminating on her distress, her love for Michael and her parents' attitude. She couldn't help wondering if things would be the same if her proposed fiancé was an officer: they were always so concerned about appearances and 'class', especially her mother.

Since she'd opened late, she only turned the shop sign to Closed for about ten minutes to eat her paste sandwiches and drink a cup of tea and she was just at the door unlocking it when she caught sight of Muriel coming down the road carrying bags of shopping. She waved and held the door open for her friend.

"Hello, Muriel, how are you?"

"Phew," sighed the other girl, sinking onto the chair near the counter.

"I'm fine but I've just come off shift and Mum wanted me to collect the shopping on the way home." She stopped for a moment and studied Lilian. "You're looking a bit peaky, girl."

That was all it took for Lilian to dissolve into tears again.

"Hey, chicken! What's the matter? Has he packed you in?"

"No, no, no! He's asked me to marry him, but – my father won't allow it!"

"Oh, I see."

"What am I going to do, Mu? I can't bear it; I just can't bear it!"

"Now, now." Muriel patted her friend's hands and lifted her chin. "Come, dry your eyes and let's talk about it properly." She went back to the shop door, turned the sign to Closed, and they went through to the little back room.

When Lilian's sobs had subsided Muriel began. "So, they won't let you marry him. Don't they like him?"

"I don't think it's that – they got on really well when he came to tea. They say it's because I'm too young and because of the war."

"Well, it's true you haven't known him very long and the war does make all our futures uncertain."

"All the more reason why we want to be together now," said Lilian sulkily.

Muriel sighed and replied, "I can see why you'd be upset but the thing is, if you're really right for each other, it won't matter if you have to wait to get married. And if he really loves you he'll be willing to wait – that's what I think."

Lilian considered all this and after a while conceded, "I suppose so."

"Now, are you seeing him tonight? 'Cos if not, you're out with me. You know the two Land Army girls over the road from us – well, one of them's got a birthday and she's having a party at the pub."

"No, I don't think so. I don't really know them."

"So you'd rather stay at home bawling and fighting with your folks, would you?"

"If you put it like that……."

"Exactly, so get your glad rags on and I'll meet you at the end of your road at 8 o'clock!"

So saying, she gathered up her shopping bags and was gone, humming a snatch of one of the new popular tunes.

The party was quite fun: most of the people there were the Land Army girls from the area who proved to be a really jolly, friendly crowd. They stayed until the end, until the landlord called time and they all spilled out into the square still singing, "One man went to mow…" which the Land Girls seemed to have adopted as their theme song.

Muriel and Lilian had both had a glass of cider and they became quite giggly on the way home; as they parted at the end of Lilian's road, Muriel gave her a little hug, saying, "You've cheered up no end, Lil. You know what they say – keep your pecker up."

"Yes," replied Lilian, "those girls are really nice and they're doing their bit for our country. It's made me think."

"Don't think too hard, girl, you'll get lines," laughed Muriel, running off with a wave.

The house was quiet as Lilian let herself in and slid the bolt across the back door. Only stopping to fill a glass of water, she crept quietly up the stairs. The top stair creaked, and as she passed her parents' door Agnes softly called out, "Goodnight dear."

Lilian didn't think she'd be able to sleep but the trauma of the last two days, the excitement of the party and the cider combined to knock her out almost as soon as her head hit the pillow. She woke early, though, and reached out to *Jane Eyre* to gently touch the wisp of grass, now very dry. Her mind turned back to the night before and how the Land Army girls seemed to share such a warm camaraderie, having a good time as well as doing war work. Although she still loved her job in the shop, since Albert had left she was often alone there for much of the day and it could get a bit lonely. Not only that, Michael was fighting and she could feel closer to him if she was doing something more active, too. By the time she got up and was dressing, Lilian had almost made up her mind to volunteer for the Land Army.

By the time she got down to the kitchen Agnes was stirring a pan of porridge and Tom had made a pot of tea and was cutting bread: he had a good eye and his slices were quite thin and very even, unlike Lilian's efforts which often tapered to a point and left the loaf a very odd shape.

Her mother was glad to see Lilian looked a lot brighter – not so down in the mouth – and she ate a decent breakfast. Lilian did not mention her idea of volunteering for the Land Army but she did tell them about the pleasant time they'd all had last night.

"They are a lively bunch, I believe, the Land Girls," commented Agnes.

"Hmph," huffed Tom. "They're a right lot if you ask me – they wolf-whistle me when I go by the fields!"

Lilian and Agnes laughed and much to Lilian's surprise, her mother said, "Well, wolf-whistle them back, then!"

The next few days were uneventful and quiet in the shop and Lilian's mood swung violently as she contemplated her future. One minute she was brimming with happiness at the memories of her lover and how sweet the times were together, hugging herself that he returned her feelings and wished to marry her; the next minute she remembered how her father had put his foot down and she was depressed again. Also she was wondering and worrying that she hadn't seen and heard from Michael for a while. Had he changed his mind?

Customers were very welcome, not only for their trade, but also to take her mind off all her troubles, and she was particularly pleased to see one of the Land Girls she met the other night. It was a good opportunity to ask about volunteering and they had a good chat about the pros and cons of the work, which gave Lilian some more food for thought. She walked to the shop door with the girl and her heart leaped as she saw Michael swinging round the corner and marching smartly towards her. Smiling joyfully at the sight of him, she threw the door open, running into his arms, careless of who might see. Clinging together they went back into the shop and after a long, passionate kiss and a deep sigh from Lilian, they began to discuss their situation.

"I have to say I was most surprised by your father's attitude," Michael began. "I thought we got on really well before but he seemed absolutely determined and I felt it was me he was objecting to."

"I can't believe they're being so horrible. Marrying you is the only thing that would make me happy – so why do they want to make me unhappy?"

"Don't cry, my darling. We'll find a way – even if we do have to wait till the end of the war."

Clutching her hankie and trying to blot her tears away, Lilian again turned the shop sign and led him into the back room, asking, "Have you got time for a cup of tea?"

"No, not really, sweetheart, but I could come back later. How about just after you close?"

"Oh, that would be wonderful – we can spend some time together."

So began the establishment of a love nest in Albert's flat.

Chapter 13

What they had called 'the Phoney War' was well and truly over: almost every day on the wireless there were accounts of bombing raids and casualties, mostly in the cities, but sometimes bombs also fell in rural areas.

When planes were heard or seen going over, the ominous roar made everyone hold their breath and often whisper a little prayer. Rationing was biting harder now, even clothing required coupons to be given up; Agnes, like many other women, was unravelling old knitted garments to be made up into something new.

Lilian's plan to join the Land Army was taking shape and she'd realised her first move must be to write to Albert so he could make plans as to the future of the shop-cum-library. It wasn't an easy letter to write but she felt sure he'd understand her feeling that she wanted to do more for the war effort. The letter was sent and the next person to tell was Michael.

Usually the two lovers did not talk much about the war or current affairs – their time together was too precious. When they did talk it was to dream about planning a future together after the war. Next time he came to the flat, though, Lilian told him she'd written to Albert and about her plans to volunteer for the Land Army. She thought he'd be pleased and supportive but he just laughed.

"You! In the Land Army – oh Lilian, darling, I don't think so!"

"Why not? What do you mean?"

"Well, it's not your kind of thing, is it? Those girls are all rough-and-ready – not your type. And the work would be too hard for you."

"Some of the girls are really nice and actually I'm quite strong enough to do farm work – I've been helping on the vegetable plot quite a lot."

He laughed again and added insult to injury, saying, "I just can't see you in wellies and shorts!"

Lilian was furious, it was their first tiff and they parted on not very good terms that day.

The very next day he arrived at the shop with a little peace offering, saying he was very sorry if he'd upset her. Afterwards, Lilian couldn't help thinking that the pleasure of making up was almost worth the quarrel. They didn't talk about the matter again and in any case Lilian thought she must wait for Albert's reply before going any further.

***

Dearest Lilian,

Thank you for your letter which finds me much improved in every way. You speak very fondly of that young man Michael; I must say I found him most pleasant and polite, too, but don't you let him break your heart.

As far as the other matter goes I can only say that you must do as your conscience feels right and of course the Land Army is a very worthy organisation. If that's what you decide to do, then the shop will have to be closed as there's no one else I would entrust it to. For myself I do not feel yet strong enough to return while we hear every day on the wireless of the bombing escalating.

Whatever you decide will be fine by me and I remain your good friend.

Warm regards

Albert

P.S. How's young Tom getting along?

***

By the time Albert's letter came, Lilian was in a quandary about her future, which in one way was about to be resolved by the announcement on the wireless that all women of working age had to sign on for approved war work. In a sense this forced Lilian's hand into telling her parents about her plans to join the Land Army.

"Oh Lilian," Agnes lamented, "I don't like to think of you having to do all those dirty, smelly jobs. And I don't know if you would be strong enough – it's such heavy work for a girl."

"I'll be strong enough, Mother. I've been helping a lot on the vegetable garden and I'm stronger than I look. Besides, if I don't do that it'll probably be factory work which I don't fancy."

"No, indeed," replied her mother. "Those factory girls can be dreadfully coarse."

Lilian smiled to herself remembering how lively the Land Army group had been and certainly not what her mother would call "top-drawer."

"I'm just popping round to see Muriel for a few minutes if she's in," said Lilian pointedly.

"Alright, dear. I didn't mean she's coarse. Muriel's a sweet girl," replied Agnes, looking rather shamefaced.

Muriel was in and the two girls had a bit of a laugh about Agnes' preconceptions.

"Mind you," laughed Muriel, "I reckon your mum's right, you might be better off in the Land Army. I'm used to factory work but it's got much harder since we've gone onto the munitions side and it's really filthy and stuffy in there most of the time. By the way, have you seen your Michael this week? Only I had a sort of a date with Jack yesterday and he didn't turn up."

"No, I haven't seen him either – I was going to ask you about them."

"More exercises, I expect – that's all they seem to do."

"Mmm, I hope that's all," said Lilian, biting her lip nervously.

One week lengthened into two, then three, then more than a month, and by this time Lilian was really anxious – he had never been away this long before. She thought about him all the time, hoping he wasn't in danger and praying for his safe return. She seemed to have lost her appetite, causing Agnes to be concerned that she might be sickening for something, but food was never wasted for Tom still retained his healthy appetite.

Each time the girls met their first topic of conversation was about Michael and Jack, although Muriel was already consoling herself with a new chap she met at the pictures.

They managed to get an afternoon together like 'the old days' to go shopping in Market Stamford. Muriel was shopping for a new outfit and Lilian was amazed at the stores she entered. Usually they looked to find something simple that you could 'dress up', but today Muriel was looking in the really classy dress shops.

"Have you come into money or something?" asked Lilian.

"Since we've been doing war work we're on a much better rate, Lil. I've been able to give me mam a bit more housekeeping and I'm still a lot better off. The war's not all bad, I can tell you."

There were two or three nice outfits that Muriel tried on and she finally chose a powder-blue two-piece with sort of rivets making a pattern on the shoulder. She handed over the coupons that were required as well and said, "Come on, let's go to our usual tea shop."

They ordered a pot of tea and cream éclairs, relaxing at their favourite table but Muriel could see that her friend wasn't really herself – quite distracted.

"Are you alright, Lil, you seem a bit down?"

She was surprised and horrified when Lilian quietly admitted, "I think I'm expecting a baby! I've missed my monthly and I've been feeling a bit sick."

Muriel gasped. "What are you gonna do? Didn't you – you know – weren't you careful?"

"I didn't think anything would happen so soon, Muriel."

"You little ninny – it only takes once and now you're in all sorts of trouble!"

"Well, I was thinking it may not be so bad because now they'll have to let us get married, won't they?"

"But he's not here and you don't know when he'll be back or IF he'll be back."

Lilian's lips wobbled as she tried to hold back tears, saying, "Don't say that – he's got to come back!"

"Sorry, Lil. I didn't mean to upset you – sure he'll be back – he'll be alright." But she wasn't sure at all.

On the way home after her heart-to-heart with Muriel, Lilian's emotions were in a turmoil. Talking to Muriel hadn't helped at all – alright for her to take such a high moral tone – she'd never been in love. Imagine how delighted Michael would be when she told him!

Taking the long way round because she was in no hurry to get home, Lilian passed the parish church and an impulse opened the pretty lych-gate and the big, wooden door into the dim feeling of sanctuary. She sat down in the nearest pew and just let the quiet calm of the old building wash over her so that after a while she felt a bit better and strong enough to put a brave face on when she got home.

Lilian didn't dare to tell her parents; if Muriel's response had been horror, she couldn't even imagine what they would say, but she knew that they would feel she'd brought shame on herself and them. If only Michael would come back they could tell them together and it wouldn't be so bad.

Next morning as soon as she got up she actually was sick for the first time and consequently arrived down at breakfast a bit late and looking rather pale. Agnes said nothing but her hawk eyes hadn't missed a thing. As soon as Tom and Edward had left for school and work she sat down opposite her daughter and demanded, "You're pregnant, aren't you!?"

Taking a breath, Lilian could only whisper, "I think so, Mother."

"You're a disgrace! Get out of my sight!"

Chapter 14

In spite of the fact that she had been concerned about Lilian for some little time, when she realised the truth, Agnes was hit by a bombshell. This was nothing that had ever entered her vision of her world: other people's daughters got pregnant and disgraced the family – not hers – not her Lilian. How could she? How could she?

The Agnes of a short time ago would have buried her head in her hands and wept but wartime Agnes had discovered a new strength in herself that enabled her to carry on with her daily routine, albeit on that day rather like an automaton. There was some washing to do, some shopping for groceries and a visit needed to one of the evacuee families where there were financial problems. After doing what she could to help the couple, who were far too proud to accept charity, Agnes made her way home to prepare a bacon pudding for their tea. While she mixed the dough and set the pudding to steam all she could think of was how she was going to tell Edward – he, too, would be totally devastated.

For once Tom and Edward arrived home at almost the same

time, giving Agnes a problem, because she felt she had to speak to her husband in confidence as soon as she could.

"Tom, would you peel some potatoes to go with the bacon pudding? – I need to speak to my husband in private."

"O.K., Mrs. Woodridge."

"Thank you, dear."

Behind her back Tom pulled a little face – she'd never called him "dear" before; although they rubbed along quite well most of the time, the lad was always aware that he could easily spark her disapproval if he wasn't careful.

Agnes led Edward towards the parlour and closed the door.

"What's the matter, dear, are you unwell?"

At last the tears she had been holding back all day would not wait any longer – tears of shame, disappointment and anger!

Edward for a moment just looked at his wife with dismay for neither of them had ever been given to displays of emotion. Feeling anxious and uncomfortable, he judged it best to say nothing until she recovered herself but just sat her down gently and patted her hand.

Sniffing and wiping her eyes with a little lace-edged hankie Agnes finally stammered, "I really d-d-don't know how to tell you. It's Lilian."

"Is she ill? Has she had an accident?" Edward was instantly alert and highly concerned.

"No, it's not that, I almost wish it were."

"Tell me, then!" Edward was now losing patience.

Agnes took a deep breath and blurted it out: "She's gone and got herself pregnant!"

For a long moment they stared at each other in disbelief, then Edward exploded with a rage Agnes had never seen him in before.

"That young soldier – I knew he was no good! Well, now they'll have to get married – what a mess – what a mess!"

"Where is she? I suppose they've done this deliberately to force our hand. What appalling behaviour!"

Agnes now became the calmer of the two and explained that she didn't think the soldier was still around because Lilian hadn't been going out much and had seemed upset.

"Whaaat do you mean! He's taken his pleasure and now cleared off?"

Agnes now slipped into anger as well: "How could she? How could she disgrace us so? I'll never be able to hold my head up in the village or the church again!"

"It's the same for me," replied Edward. "All the bank customers will know and be sniggering about us. It's just unforgivable!"

By this time the potatoes were cooked and Tom had mashed them using the big metal masher, adding a tiny bit of butter and some pepper as Lilian had shown him. Now he didn't know what to do and on hearing raised voices from the parlour he knew better than to interrupt. The very fact of hearing angry noises had surprised him, though he was familiar enough with such scenarios at home from neighbours and even his mum; in the Woodridge house he had never heard anyone raising their voice – what could be up?

Just then, Lilian came into the kitchen through the back door and Tom noticed at once that she seemed to be in a bit of a state, too. There was no time to enquire, for Agnes, having heard her daughter's footsteps, called out, "Lilian, come here at once!"

This time, Tom crept into the hall to listen and soon realised what was causing all the pandemonium. Before long, Lilian was sobbing and it was clear that Mr. and Mrs. Woodridge were absolutely furious mainly because of what others would think. Finally Lilian burst out of the parlour and ran upstairs to her bedroom in floods of tears. The last thing Tom heard Edward say was: "We'll have to send her away – we can't have her here."

No one ate much supper that evening, tasty as it was, and Tom was glad to go up to his room to do some homework and get away from the oppressive atmosphere of angry silence.

Feeling really worried about her friend, Muriel decided to take the bull by the horns and marched up the path to knock on the Woodridges' door. It was opened, as she had expected, by a stony-faced Agnes who merely turned away and called up the stairs, "Muriel's here. Are you coming down?"

After a few awkward minutes, while Muriel didn't know whether to stay or go, Lilian ran down the stairs pulling on a jacket.

"Hello, Mu. Let's go for a walk."

The girls linked arms and hurried down the lane for fifty yards or so before Muriel spoke: "You told them, then?"

"Actually Mother guessed," Lilian admitted.

"Yes, I thought she might," said Muriel. "And are they supporting you?"

Tears again welled in Lilian's eyes as she went through the anger and rejection she'd experienced from her parents.

"And the worst thing is I went up to the camp and there's no one there anymore, only a couple of sentries who said they've all gone and couldn't tell me anything. Maybe I'll never see him again, Muriel. If I can't marry him my parents want to send me away."

"Oh chicken, what a mess! Listen, I was thinking, one of the girls in the factory had the same thing and she managed to get rid of it – she took some kind of herbal pills and had a hot bath. Shall I ask her what she took?"

"Oh no, Muriel, I couldn't do that – it's part of Michael and me, I just couldn't, and anyway that's wicked – you know it is."

"Well, it's just an idea."

"I don't know what to do," murmured Lilian, crying again.

"Mother says I'll never get married now because no one else will want me."

At length they turned round and walked back, Muriel still trying to comfort her friend but with little success.

***

It was the following Friday night – Agnes was knitting and dozing gently in front of the dwindling parlour fire and the young people had completed a jigsaw puzzle on the kitchen table and gone to bed – when Edward returned from the pub slightly the worse for wear and relaxed into his chair.

Glancing up, Agnes registered a seemingly satisfied look on her husband's face and remarked, "You're looking pleased with yourself tonight."

"I don't know that 'pleased' is the right word but I have

something to tell you."

"Oh, what's that?"

"I've just come from having a drink with our future son-in-law."

Agnes gasped and dropped several stitches. "What do you mean?"

"Just that my good friend Desmond has offered to make an honest woman of Lilian by marrying her and taking her to his home in Ireland."

"Well, that's a turn-up! But do you think she'll agree?"

"She'll have to: as far as I can see it's the only way. She'll have to do what she is told."

What Edward didn't tell Agnes was that he had promised Desmond Blackstock several hundred pounds, almost all of their savings, to pay off his debts and set them up in a new home.

***

It was a quiet wedding even by wartime standards: noon at the Registry Office in Market Stanford with just Lilian's parents as witnesses. Lilian wore a silver grey costume with a pink corsage – no veil, no long, white dress that she might have dreamed of long ago. She made the responses required of her clearly in an emotionless monotone. There was to be no wedding breakfast as the newly-weds had to go straight to the station to catch the connection for the evening boat train. Walking back down the steps of the Registry, Lilian realised she felt numb from head to toe, inside and out. Goodbyes were said on the pavement and though both women had tears in their eyes, the rift between mother and daughter was too wide to heal – there had been too much anger, shame and recrimination in the last few weeks.

Just as the taxi arrived one little ray of sunshine arrived in the shape of Muriel, running along the road clutching a little bag of confetti which she tossed over the couple, much to Agnes' disapproval.

Lilian hugged her friend, ignoring the open taxi door and whispered, "Thank you so much for coming, Mu."

"I couldn't let you go without saying goodbye, could I? Now you make sure you keep in touch. Write to me, won't you?!"

"I will, Mu, I promise. Goodbye."

Straight away she was bundled into the taxi and it trundled off to the station. Looking back at the little group on the pavement, Lilian waved and wondered if she would ever see them again.

Part 2

Chapter 15

The Irish Sea played its usual tricks, making the crossing quite choppy and Lilian was very seasick the whole way. Desmond, a good sailor, was fine and, although he was kind to his new, young wife in a formal sort of way there was, truth to be told, little he could do to help. She'd only been on a little riverboat before and had no idea she would feel so wretched. For hours she longed for this misery to be over and at one point even began to long for her life to be over, what with the seasickness and the awful knowledge that she had been forced to marry a man she did not love. She knew that it was a sin, however, and tried to remember that the voyage would be soon over; the marriage wouldn't be, though.

At last the ferry gained the calmer waters of the harbour, the horizon stopped pitching up and down, and Lilian quickly began to feel more human.

The first thing they did after disembarking and organising the luggage was to head for the nearest hostelry for breakfast. Lilian wasn't sure she'd feel like eating much but Desmond answered her, "You'll feel much better with a good Irish breakfast in you."

The breakfast was actually quite delicious: thick, local bacon, fresh eggs and tasty soda bread with creamy butter. Lilian couldn't remember when she'd had such a scrumptious meal, all polished off with a pot of tea while Desmond, to her surprise, washed his meal down with a pint of Guinness.

"Isn't there rationing in Ireland, like at home?" she wondered.

"Oh yes, there is," replied Desmond, "but there's always a way round these things." She would soon come to realise that her husband had adopted this phrase as his mantra.

Next they had to hurry to the station to catch the train to Dundalk. As it chugged through the outskirts of the city, stone and brick quickly gave way to leafy fields and rolling countryside which Lilian would have really enjoyed if it hadn't been for the persistent feeling that every mile was taking her further from everything she had known and loved. The track wound along the coast revealing beautiful, lonely beaches and secluded coves; how she would have loved to walk hand in hand with Michael exploring the shore: No! No! Don't think about that – that way lies madness!

Before long the stress and exhaustion of the last twenty-four hours caught up with her and, covering herself with her coat as a blanket, she fell into a deep sleep only to be woken by Desmond shaking her and saying, "The next stop is ours and it's only a halt so it won't be stopping long." This meant they had to get themselves and the luggage ready to disembark and it seemed to be making Desmond very anxious. Surely he should be looking forward to reaching his home and seeing his parents, thought Lilian, but his tension was apparent in the nervous way he began to smoke his cigarettes one after the other.

The train drew to a shuddering halt and sure enough it was a tiny station where no one else disembarked. There was a pony and trap waiting, which seemed odd but perhaps it meets every train, thought Lilian. Desmond loaded on the luggage and gave directions to the driver without any comment to his wife.

The trap set off at a leisurely pace which inevitably seemed to annoy Desmond.

"Can't this thing go any faster?" he demanded of the driver.

"Ach, she generally likes to go at her own pace," replied the man, giving the reins a bit of a shake. The creature shook its head once or twice but made no effort to increase its pace – it was quite clear she'd no intention of hurrying.

The ride seemed to go on for ever. A light drizzle had started, really more of a soft mist than rain, but still enough to dampen hair and clothes and put a sheen on the pony's coat. Lilian was tempted to ask how much further they had to go, but the grim look on Desmond's face did not encourage conversation, and anyway she supposed it would sound childish.

At last, on the next rise, a large country mansion came into view and as she wondered if that was where they were heading, the cart veered sharply to the left and drew up in front of a much more modest but still handsome lodge. It was a sturdy, double-fronted building in reasonable repair, although the front gate had swung open and was leaning against a large and unkempt hedge. The small front garden was clearly in need of some care.

Desmond jumped down from the trap, leaving Lilian to follow and the driver to begin unloading the luggage. The lane was deserted as he knocked quite loudly on the front door. The sound seemed to echo around in quite an eerie way. By the time Lilian joined him on the step he was banging the knocker again. Perhaps his parents are deaf, Lilian thought, or perhaps there's no one in.

Just then the door was eased open a crack and a surprised face took in the visitors. For a few seconds nothing was said, then the old man wiped Lilian's tentative smile from her face by growling, "Oh it's you. What do you want?"

"Good to see you, too, Father," Desmond replied with a good attempt at hale and hearty bluster. When there was no reply, he introduced Lilian and asked if they could come in.

"No, I don't think so," replied the old man.

"Well, can I see Mother, then?" asked Desmond. "I'm sure she'd like to meet my new wife."

"Your mother's been dead this twelve-month, boy. She died of shame – the shame you brought upon us – so you're not welcome in this house ever again. Go away!"

So saying, he shut the door and they could hear bolts being drawn inside. Desmond was clearly furious – he kicked the gate further into the hedge and went back to the trap.

"What are we going to do?" asked Lilian.

"We'll go into the village and find somewhere to stay," he replied. "Don't worry, I'll sort out the old eejit later."

Perhaps his father was deranged, thought Lilian, as they clambered back into the trap, hoping they would be able to find somewhere – anywhere – to stay. At this point she was so exhausted she just needed to rest somewhere that didn't rattle or jolt or float, and a cup of tea.

The trap driver didn't seem a bit surprised but didn't forget to mention that the village was a bit further so it would cost more. This, of course, added to Desmond's already furious temper.

The village was quiet in the gathering gloom: some curtains were already drawn against the dark, autumn chill while some windows showed a little light, affording glimpses of the homely life within.

The driver pulled up outside the village pub and Desmond jumped straight down and disappeared into it without a backward glance; Lilian was left to clamber down and follow him in, carrying her own overnight bag while the driver, disgruntled by this time, threw the rest of the luggage onto the pavement and went in to collect his fare. Desmond was already downing a pint of Guinness with a whiskey chaser and took little notice of Lilian until the barman nodded to her, saying, "And this'd been the young lady in question, I'm guessin." After a few minutes she gratefully gathered that there was a room available for the night and quite soon the landlady appeared to show her the way. Colleen McBride was a hefty, middle-aged woman with iron-grey hair, ruddy cheeks and a ready smile; she wore her sleeves rolled up, revealing strong forearms and washday-red hands.

"Come this way, dearie," she began, grabbing the small case from her and marched ahead.

"I'm sure yous'ell be comfortable here, it's our best room you've got."

Lilian smiled her thanks and murmured a compliment although it was a very basic room with a double bed, one chair, one table and a wash-hand basin.

"You look all in, my dear. Why don't you unpack your few things and I'll be bringing you a cup o' tea."

"Oh that would be lovely, thank you," replied Lilian as she sank onto the edge of the bed.

Colleen returned a short time later with a pot of tea and some biscuits, a long list of directions as to the use of the water heater in the bathroom, and the information that every bath would cost an extra sixpence. It didn't matter to Lilian at that moment for she was far too tired to do anything but fall straight into bed after her very welcome tea.

Just as she was falling asleep she felt a funny little jolt below her waist just near the hip, not a pain but just a sort of nudge – there it was again. After a moment she realised it was the first movement she had felt of the baby growing in her womb. She smiled and put her hand over the place it had been, thinking at once of her lost lover. Over the previous weeks she had trained herself not to dwell too much on what might have been, realising that getting upset would be bad for the child, but it now struck her as a cruel twist of fate that she should feel that precious movement first while lying in what was effectively the marriage bed of another man.

It was very late by the time Desmond stumbled into the room and fell, half-dressed, into bed. Lilian was in such a deep sleep that she barely registered his presence until she was woken by sunlight penetrating the thin curtains. Not wanting to wake him, she slid carefully out of bed, dressed quietly and, realising she was very hungry, made her way to the kitchen, where Colleen was frying sausages and toasting soda bread.

The woman greeted her in a really friendly way, motioned her to sit at the rough, wooden table and in moments put down a steaming cup of tea followed by a big plate of sausage, egg and toast.

"Ah, come now, will you'se get that down ya? I can see you need building up, and this will start your day with something warm inside you."

Lilian had indeed lost a good deal of weight due to the stress of recent weeks and she rather hoped that was what Colleen referred to, rather than her pregnancy, which she was still rather shy about. The breakfast was most welcome and she polished off every morsel, thinking for a moment of how young Tom used to relish his food and finish up everything in sight.

"That was really delicious, thank you."

"It's a pleasure cooking for someone that really enjoys their food, ma dear. How about another cup of tea?"

The two women sat a while over the tea, chatting casually until Colleen asked: "Da ya think himself'll be down soon, only I've some errands so maybe I could leave you to fix his breakfast – if that's alright."

Lilian didn't want to admit that she'd no idea when he'd be down so she quickly replied, "Oh that's fine, you go and I'll clear up these things as well."

"What a good girl you are! Thank you, my dear."

Lilian was glad of the homely task to occupy her and she was actually humming softly when Desmond came into the kitchen.

"Didn't hear you get up," he growled.

"Colleen's had to go out; she left me to get your breakfast. What would you like? There's sausages and eggs."

"No! I don't want any of that. Just give me a cup of tea and I'll be getting a hair o' the dog."

She wasn't entirely sure what he meant so poured the tea and sat down again as he wandered through into the bar.

She expected that later they would go into the village or the nearest town to find somewhere to live but when she went to find him he'd disappeared. She thought he may have gone house-hunting by himself and decided that she'd go for a walk to explore the village, rather than sit alone in the room all day. It was a crisp autumn morning with golden leaves tumbling from the trees in a playful breeze. Lilian was glad of her hat and gloves and delighted that, as she walked past the few shops in the village, perfect strangers greeted her with 'Top o' the morning'. Everyone seemed really friendly.

At the end of the main street a little stream babbled beside the road and a bench had been thoughtfully placed beside it. From there she could see across lightly wooded downs to blue/grey hills beyond. After a short time a young woman with a pram came to share the bench with her. The girl introduced herself as Aileen and they chatted easily, mainly about her gorgeous little baby boy. Lilian immediately imagined herself wheeling her own precious babe and for the first time began to actually look forward to the prospect. The child began to fuss and Aileen said she'd need to get him home for his feed. As they left, Lilian hoped they'd find somewhere to live nearby as she felt sure they could become good friends.

Desmond didn't return until late and Lilian had eaten nothing but an apple all day. Colleen kindly brought Lilian some soup when she realised her husband seemed unaware of the situation. Lilian stayed awake until he came to bed, hoping he would say he'd found them a home but he made no comment and quickly fell asleep, snoring loudly.

The pattern was repeated for several days until Lilian decided to tackle him one morning at breakfast. He didn't seem to take her concerns on-board until she reminded him that they were paying almost hotel prices at the inn.

"Alright, alright. I'll find somewhere today – it can't be very difficult," grumbled Desmond as he was leaving.

"Shall I come with you?"

"No!"

He returned later the same day and virtually ordered Lilian to pack up their things as they were moving straight away. As she packed and tidied as best she could, a vociferous quarrel came from downstairs, where Desmond appeared to be arguing about the bill. He was in a vile mood when he came back and hustled her out without even a chance to say goodbye to Colleen.

Their belongings were piled into a handcart and they set off down the street towards the edge of the village and along a muddy track to a narrow alley where dirty children played and old men coughed and stared. They stopped at the end of a shabby terrace and Lilian saw with dismay the hovel that would be her home for the next few years.

Chapter 16

First sight of the shabby, end-of terrace cottage plunged Lilian into despair. She hadn't expected a palace but she (and her parents) had certainly been led to believe that the future held much better prospects than this. Seeing the look of horror on her face, Desmond was at first defensive but then rapidly shifted to belligerent. "Well, what did you expect? It's not easy to find somewhere, you know. Anyway, it's only what you deserve in the circumstances – all the trouble you've caused!" It was the first time he'd reproached her in that way and it felt like a slap in the face.

The front door opened directly from the street and it creaked alarmingly as they entered. Desmond nastily joked, "I hope you don't expect me to carry you across the threshold!"

Inside there were just two rooms downstairs and two upstairs – it was cold and musty and the general air of dereliction pervaded. It was sparsely furnished and a veil of dust lay everywhere; clearly it hadn't been inhabited for some time. The small backyard had the outside privy, a washing line, a rusty old bedstead, and the one good thing was a well-stocked woodpile.

In silence they unloaded the cart and Desmond immediately left to return it. For two pins Lilian could have sat at the rough, wooden kitchen table and cried but her pride and upbringing gave her the backbone to set to and try to make the place habitable, if not homely. They had passed a small corner shop streets away so she set off there to purchase some cleaning materials and a few basic provisions.

The shop in question was the sort that sells everything you can think of, but stores it all in a great big muddle. Mr. and Mrs. O'Leary, the proprietors, greeted Lilian the moment she stepped in the door, immediately recognising that she was new to the village. In spite of herself, Lilian couldn't help smiling at the sight of them for she couldn't make up her mind whether they reminded her more of the 'Jack Sprat' nursery rhyme or a saucy seaside postcard: Mrs. O'Leary was large and comfortable in a jolly sort of way, while her husband, you'd have to admit, was a scrawny little specimen.

Lilian's shopping took quite some time, for each item had to be searched for among the many shelves and boxes, and the process was continually punctuated by well-meaning chatter and gossip. The purchases were piled into a couple of boxes and Patrick O'Leary called his errand boy from the back room to help carry the shopping. Walking back to the house with the young man reminded Lilian painfully of times she'd spent with young Tom – life had been so carefree then.

Back indoors, Lilian managed to get the range alight and with a good deal of dusting and scrubbing the back room at any rate felt quite cosy. Realising she was very hungry, she next put together a simple meal and sat down to eat when, to her surprise the front door opened and Desmond appeared carrying a rabbit carcase and two bottles of stout.

"Oh, you've made something to eat! Well, that's good: the rabbit will do for tomorrow, then."

Desmond polished off the two bottles of stout with the meal and was soon nodding in the chair. Then quite early he went off to bed, leaving his wife to clear up.

Lilian first moved the rabbit off the draining board into the larder, thinking it would be the coolest place and also she didn't have to look at it while she washed up and, indeed, until she fell asleep later, she couldn't get out of her mind the prospect of having to deal with the poor creature tomorrow.

Unusually in the morning Desmond was up and out early, saying he didn't know what time he'd be back. After a simple breakfast of toast and tea Lilian set to on cleaning the rest of the house, mainly in order to put off the task of skinning and jointing the rabbit.

Eventually she realised she couldn't put it off any longer so she fetched it from the larder to the kitchen table and laid out some newspaper, while she had tried to decide on the best way to tackle it – a task she'd never really dreamed of before: at home the butcher had always prepared the meat. Taking a deep breath, she decided the first requirement would be a nice, sharp knife, so she took the only knife she had to the back step and proceeded to sharpen it as she had seen her mother do sometimes. After a short time Lilian could feel eyes upon her and, looking round, she saw a small face peering through a hole in the fence from next door.

"Hello," said Lilian.

The child didn't reply for a moment but then asked, "What are you doing?"

"I'm sharpening this knife."

"Why?"

Lilian didn't want to say she was intending or hoping to skin a rabbit with it so she just replied. "Because I need a nice, sharp knife."

That seemed to satisfy the little girl who decided to introduce herself: "My name's Siobhan. What's yours?"

"I'm Lilian. It's nice to meet you, Siobhan, now that we're neighbours."

The knife seemed to have a decent edge now so Lilian stood up and went back indoors, not expecting the child to follow her. But she did, squeezing through the gap in the fence and standing in the doorway.

"Oh, you've got a rabbit!" she cried, grinning. "Can I have the skin?"

"What do you want the skin for?"

"The ragbag man gives you threepence if they're in good nick."

"Oh really?"

Just at that moment they both heard a call from next door, "Siobhan, where are you?"

The little girl ran out, calling, "I'm here, Mum, come and see, Lilian's got a rabbit."

A few moments later an attractive young woman appeared through the back gate. She was petite, with masses of tumbling, dark curls and the piercing blue eyes and pale skin so typical of the Irish Celts.

"I hope she hasn't been bothering you," was her opening remark as she took hold of her daughter's hand as though to lead her away.

"No, no," protested Lilian, "we've been having a little chat and she's interested in that!" Lilian pointed to the dead rabbit on the newspaper-covered kitchen table and grimaced.

"Do you want a hand with that?" the young woman offered immediately.

"Oh, I would be so grateful," sighed Lilian. "To tell the truth I don't even know where to start. But shall we have a cup of tea first. There's some in the pot – it'll just need warming."

Once that was done they moved the rabbit aside and chatted easily while Siobhan played happily with a home-made game of five stones using smooth pebbles.

"I've heard your name is Lilian, mine's Maura."

"That's a really pretty name and it's quite like the English name of Muriel. My best friend at home was called Muriel."

In the course of their conversation Lilian learned that Maura was a widow with three children, the eldest two already at school. Her husband had been a merchant seaman and his boat was torpedoed early in the war.

"Oh I'm so sorry to hear that," said Lilian, reaching over to touch the girl's hand and reflecting for a moment that they had a sadness in common, having lost someone they loved.

Maura managed a little grin and replied, "I've had to be strong for the kids, they keep me going. So come on, let's get at this critter." She was clearly quite experienced at the task and in no time at all the creature was skinned and the pelt put aside for cleaning. She then showed Lilian how to dismember and joint it ready for the pot. It was quite a large, meaty buck so there was really more than Lilian needed and she was glad to be able to share the pieces as a thankyou to Maura for her invaluable help.

As she led Siobhan by the hand back out of the gate Maura called out, "Come round if you need anything, Lilian. Sure you'll soon be settled in!"

To prepare the rabbit stew some vegetables would be needed so Lilian got ready to pop out to the little corner shop, humming as she did so and realising that was the first time she had done so for a long time. What a pleasure to find such a nice girl next door and her resemblance to Muriel was remarkable – not in looks but her name and her cheerful, down-to-earth manner. Maybe later, when she'd come to terms with this Irish lifestyle, she would write and tell Muriel about Maura.

An onion and a few carrots and potatoes all went into the pot with the rabbit pieces and Lilian set it on the range to gently cook away. Next she decided to tackle the front room and give it a good spring clean. The furniture was old and shabby, nothing like what she had been used to; everything was covered in dust and cobwebs where an army of spiders must have invaded. Fortunately Lilian was never one to be bothered about spiders, especially since most of these seemed to have perished long ago.

After a couple of hours the room looked a bit better and felt fresher – tomorrow she would wash the thin curtains, hoping they didn't fall apart. Having stopped work, Lilian realised she was exhausted and hungry so she went to the kitchen to check on the stew and make a cup of tea. There was a little bit of stale soda bread left from yesterday so she ate that with her tea thinking she would have some stew when Desmond returned.

Before long, she'd dozed off sitting by the warm range and didn't wake until it was almost dark. The stew smelled quite appetising so she thought maybe she wouldn't wait for Desmond but just as she was lighting a couple of lamps she heard his key in the door. He looked in a good mood – Lilian had quickly learned to gauge his moods: there was something about his set of features. His only greeting was: "I hope there's some food, I'm starving."

"I made a stew with the rabbit," replied Lilian.

"Let's have it, then," he said, plonking himself down at the table to be waited on.

The stew was really good, especially with the gravy mopped up with soda bread. The couple ate in silence and Desmond made no comment on the food. Lilian thought of telling him how Maura had helped her skin and joint the rabbit but decided against it: good mood or not, he might not have wanted a neighbour in the house.

As soon as they were finished Lilian began to clear away and Desmond rose, saying, "I'm going straight to bed for I've an early start in the morning."

Lilian looked up from the sink. "Have you got a job, then?" she asked.

"Job! No. Jobs are for small people. I've got a business opportunity."

Chapter 17

Siobhan must have been peeping through the fence because as soon as Lilian carried a basket of washing into the yard to hang up she appeared, squeezing through the gap.

"Top o' the morning, Lilian," she grinned.

"Top o' the morning, Siobhan," smiled Lilian.

"Mammy says I mustn't bother you in the house but I can bother you in the yard, can't I?"

"You're not bothering me, Siobhan; it's nice to see your smiling face."

The little girl grinned again and held up what she was carrying. "What have you got there, Siobhan?"

"This is what I got with the rabbit skin money. I got three pencils, a writing book and a lollipop, but I've eaten the lollipop."

"That's nice – the book will keep you busy."

"Yes, I like drawing AND I'm learning to write my name."

"Are you? That's very clever."

Quite forgetting, or ignoring, her mother's instruction, Siobhan followed Lilian back into the house and sat down at the kitchen table. Swinging her legs back and forth she asked, "What are you going to do now?"

"I'm going to make some pastry for a homity pie," replied Lilian, getting out the bowl and spooning flour into it.

"What's a homity pie?"

"It's a kind of pie made with potato and onion."

"Can I help?"

"Well, I tell you what, if you wash your hands really well you can have the leftover pastry to make some biscuits."

"Oh good, I love biscuits."

Siobhan ran to the sink, but realising she wouldn't be able to reach properly she began to pull the chair she had been sitting on, over.

"Put your book and pencils on the dresser first, Siobhan, in case we get flour or pastry on them."

The little girl did exactly as she was told and washed her hands really thoroughly before joining Lilian at the kitchen table, watching carefully and waiting impatiently for her share of the pastry.

With pie in the oven Siobhan stationed herself at the kitchen table while Lilian rolled her sleeves up for her. At that moment the baby made its presence felt with a little tremor and in her mind's eye Lilian could see herself doing the self-same thing with her little girl in a few years' time; she began to feel sure that she was carrying a girl.

Siobhan brought her back to the present with "How do you make biscuits, then?"

"Well, we'll roll out the pastry and sprinkle some sugar on it first; then roll it out again and cut it into shapes. What shapes do you like?"

Siobhan was too busy rolling to think about the shapes yet. The biscuit-making became very messy but was lots of fun and soon they were ready for the oven. After clearing the kitchen table they needed something to do to stop Siobhan opening the oven door every few moments, so they sat down with the pencil and notebook to practise some letters.

The next challenge when the biscuits were out of the oven was to stop Siobhan tasting them until they were cool enough to eat. When Lilian declared they were ready, the little girl politely offered her one first but she declined, suspecting they would be very hard, bearing in mind the number of times they were rolled out. Siobhan, however, happily crunched on and was about to start on another when Lilian said, "Better only eat one just now, Siobhan, or you'll spoil your dinner. Tell you what, we'll put the rest in a little bag and you can take them home to share with Mummy and your brother and sister."

"Oh yes, and I can say I made them all by myself – I did, didn't I?"

"You certainly did most of the work," laughed Lilian.

Siobhan ran off happily clutching her latest achievements as Lilian reflected that she'd felt happier this morning than she had for months.

Desmond's business dealings were his only priority and took up all of his time, his outings becoming more and more irregular, often keeping him out until very late; a couple of evenings he didn't even return until Lilian was in bed. One particular night she woke to hear him stumbling up the stairs and could smell the rank odour of whiskey before he even entered the room. For some reason he started to sing a ribald song as he undressed and then slumped into bed beside her. For the first time ever he rolled over to say goodnight but Lilian winced and pulled away at his touch. "Oh don't worry," he snarled. "I won't be touching you while you're carrying the soldier's bastard."

"Don't say such a thing," whispered Lilian, but there was no reply for he'd fallen into a drunken stupor. Lilian buried her face in the pillow to keep back the tears that threatened, and managed to sleep after a while.

Next morning Desmond appeared to have forgotten all about his cruel words and in fact was quite expansive, offering her some housekeeping money and saying that the 'business' was starting to come good. Lilian was glad of the money as she only had a little left of the gift her father had given her on the last day; she decided to put some of this cash aside for things the baby would need but didn't mention that to her husband.

Lilian hadn't seen Maura for a few days and would rather like to see her to ask for some tips on making soda bread: she had tried a couple of times but it didn't seem to come out right. She was just thinking about going out to peep over the backyard fence to see if her neighbour was about, when a knock came at the back door and there was Maura holding a large cardboard box.

"Hello, Maura, come in. What have you got there?"

"Phew," gasped Maura, dumping the box on the table. "I've been having a sort-out and I'm thinking these things are going to be useful to you – I'm certainly not going to need them again."

Taking in the contents of the box, Lilian could see it was full of baby clothes and maternity smocks.

Blushing slightly she said, "How did you know?"

"Lilian, I've had three of my own. You get to know the signs and besides, you are 'blossoming' a bit, you know."

"I suppose I am," admitted Lilian, cradling the small bump of her stomach.

"Well, come on, get the kettle on and let's have some tea while you unpack the box!"

"Oh, this is really exciting. You are so kind, Maura."

Lilian soon busied herself with filling the kettle and putting it to boil as she asked, "Where's Siobhan today?"

"There's no school today so Sian, that's my eldest, has taken her to the park in the village for a while. He's ever so good with her and since they've got no daddy now he often says he's got to be the man of the family." A sob hitched her last word and Lilian turned to see tears running down her friend's face.

"Sorry," whispered Maura. "I don't normally talk on like this. It's just it would have been Patrick's birthday today. Times like this I really miss him."

Lilian crossed to her friend and stroked her back while Maura fished a hankie from her apron pocket and taking a deep breath, said, "I'm alright now, dear. Where's that tea?"

It didn't take long for Lilian to brew the tea and place two steaming cups on the table. Between sips of tea Lilian proceeded to unpack the box. On top were three maternity smocks and a loose, elastic-waisted skirt. The tops weren't really the colours she would have chosen but they were quite pretty and of good-quality fabrics. She held each one up against herself for Maura's approval, and declared, "They'll fit you just fine and they've worn really well because Patrick always insisted on buying the best we could afford." She sighed and looked into the distance, taking a little trip down memory lane. "He was a good provider and always did his best for us. We weren't well off but we were comfortable. It was a lot easier to manage then, than it is now. With just his pension coming in it's a problem really for things like the children's clothes and shoes. Still, I suppose everyone has to pull their belts in these days; everyone except you of course – you've got to let yours out." She winked cheekily and both girls burst out laughing.

"As soon as Siobhan goes to school," Maura continued, "I shall look for a part-time job – get a little extra cash and get out of the house a bit."

Lilian topped up their tea and in between cooing over the baby clothes – so tiny and mostly in neutral colours so suitable for boy or girl – she came up with an idea.

"Maura, if you get work before Siobhan is at school I'll gladly look after her. After all, I'm not going anywhere for quite a while." She patted her abdomen. "And if you know anyone who could lend me a sewing machine I'll gladly stitch or alter clothes for you. I'm quite good at needlework and it's usually much cheaper than buying ready-made."

"Well, that'd be great, Lilian, I well may take you up on that," smiled Maura.

Lilian finished unpacking the box and put it by the back door while Maura finished her tea and stood to go. Before leaving she enquired, "Have you booked a midwife yet? How long have you got to go?"

Maura sat down again and assumed a schoolmarmish tone: "You need to get things in place. It's no good leaving it all to the last minute. If you like I can introduce you to a midwife I know quite well."

"I don't know anyone around here, so that would be great."

"That's settled, then – we'll go round to meet Mrs. Flaherty one day next week." Pausing for a moment she then asked, "Your husband won't think I'm interfering, though, will he?"

"Oh no, he won't mind; he's not really inter-est-ed." Lilian's voice tailed off, realising what she'd said.

Maura said nothing; just a little frown clouded her face as though she didn't quite understand.

"I'll tell you all about it one day, Maura, but I can't just yet." She searched her friend's face for signs of derision or disgust but saw none. "Have I shocked you?"

"It's none of my business," replied Maura. "I'm not about to judge you and you can be sure as far as I'm concerned it never leaves this kitchen."

"Thank you – I appreciate that."

Maura grasped the other girl's hand in a gesture of real friendship and support, then seeing that Lilian was close to tears, she resumed in a businesslike manner: "You'll like Mrs. Flaherty. She delivered all three of mine. She's very down-to-earth and she doesn't have any truck with men about the place – thinks they just get in the way. But that won't be a problem for you, will it?"

"No, it won't!"

Chapter 18

"Where did all this come from!?" roared Desmond.

Lilian hadn't heard him come in: she was upstairs trying on the maternity clothes and surprising herself in some ways that she was actually taking an interest and some pride in the way she looked, for the first time in ages. She immediately realised he was angry about the baby clothes for some reason, so she hurried down to the kitchen.

"They're from Maura. She doesn't need them anymore so she kindly passed them on."

"Who the hell's Maura?"

"Our next-door neighbour. I told you, Desmond."

"Hmph, what is it with women that you've gotta keep talk, talk, talking? I don't want her knowing all our business so you just keep clear of her! Understand?!"

Lilian could see he'd been drinking again and she didn't want a row, so she just nodded and he seemed satisfied.

Reaching into his pocket, he drew out a flask and took a swig before demanding, "What's for supper?"

"Stew," replied Lilian, turning to stir it and get out the cutlery.

"Stew again! Can't you get anything decent?"

"Well, I didn't know what time you'd be back and it's the easiest to keep warm."

"I won't be going out tomorrow – I've got a few things to do indoors, so get a chop or steak or something."

"I'll do my best," sighed Lilian, "but there's rationing here as well, you know."

"Oh there's ways and means," growled Desmond, dismissing her comment.

Lilian didn't eat much: she found she rarely had much appetite these days but did manage a small portion, knowing how important it was for the healthy development of the babe. Desmond tucked into the stew with relish, washing it down with more of the flask contents. Although Lilian had finished long before him, she remained seated until he laid down his cutlery, still keeping to the polite manners that Agnes had instilled in her for all those years.

After clearing away, Lilian gathered up the baby things and took them upstairs to the small bedroom where there was an old chest, really a blanket box, but she thought it would be a nice place to store the little layette which she hoped to add to in the coming weeks. Desmond, meanwhile, settled himself comfortably by the range, musing that the stew had actually been quite tasty considering it didn't have much meat. Mind you, he thought, Rory's poteen tends to improve the taste of anything – he makes a really good brew. Sipping from the flask again he reflected how getting to know Rory had been a real stroke of luck.

He was landlord of the furthest pub in the village and a relative newcomer to the area, which was why he had no idea about Desmond's rather murky past.

He had welcomed him as a new and potentially good customer, introducing him to the group of 'regulars', letting him build up a 'slate', and even offering a loan when he had a big loss on the horses that time. The delivery and collection jobs that Desmond had gladly undertaken were dead easy and he'd never had any problems across the border. Alright, it probably wasn't altogether legal, but as Rory said, "It does'na hurt anybody and it's easy money."

Desmond slept late next morning and Lilian was already ironing in the kitchen when he clattered half-dressed down the stairs and stood in the doorway for a moment, as if gathering strength for the next stage; his eyes were red and his skin quite grey. Lilian politely wished him "Good morning," receiving only a grunt for a reply. He was a long time in the privy and when he emerged he went straight to the sink, drank a cup of water and washed in cold water.

"Are you ill?" asked Lilian as he sat down at the table, drying his face on the kitchen towel. He shook his head, then groaned slightly because that made the headache worse.

"Do you want any breakfast?"

"No, I'll just have a cup of tea if there's any going."

For quite a long time he sat morosely sipping the tea and promising himself to avoid Rory's poteen in future – it seemed great when you were drinking it, put fire in your belly, but it sure packed a mule's punch next morning.

When he felt a bit better he staggered back upstairs, finished dressing and decided to go out without bothering with a shave. The pubs wouldn't be open yet, but maybe that little corner shop would have some beer to take the edge off his awful thirst; anyway, he needed a bit of shopping from there to ensure their business merchandise could be kept safe.

Somehow the O'Learys in the shop seemed to think they knew him already, greeting him in a rather overfriendly way and enquiring after his 'grand young wife'. Then he realised that of course Lilian had been in here gossiping as well – this would really have to stop.

They didn't have any beer but they had some cider and a miniature of brandy that the old woman said they kept "for medical purposes". The other items he required were a padlock with hasp and some screws which were all available but took an age in the finding. Desmond was becoming increasingly impatient for the transaction to be concluded and for his drink; at last he paid and took a swig of the brandy while he waited for his change.

Back at home he went straight into the front room, started on the cider and began the job of fixing the hasp to the fitted cupboard beside the fireplace.

Lilian, who was ironing in the kitchen, heard him come in and wondered briefly what he was doing in the front room. After a time there came the sounds of banging and swearing so her curiosity got the better of her and she peeped in to see him kneeling at the cupboard with one shoe off (the banging) and red in the face, trying to fix the screws with his penknife.

Returning to the kitchen and the pile of ironing, she thought for a moment before putting the flat iron aside and popping next door.

She tapped on the back door and went in, as Maura always did.

"Good morning, Lilian." She was greeted immediately. "What can I do for you?"

"Would you have such a thing as a screwdriver, Maura? Himself is trying to fix screws with a penknife."

Both women smiled not only at the picture it conjured up, but also at Lilian already picking up something of an Irish accent.

Maura briefly rummaged in a kitchen drawer and produced a small screwdriver with the air of a music hall magician.

"Oh, thanks, Maura, I'll bring it straight back when he's done."

"No hurry at all," smiled her friend.

Lilian didn't say anything, just entered the front room and held out the screwdriver to where Desmond, still on his knees, was finishing the bottle of cider.

"Where d'yer get that, then?" he scowled.

"Borrowed it from Maura."

"Hmph, thought I told you not to get so thick with her," he muttered, taking the little tool and bending to the cupboard again.

Lilian just returned to her ironing, wondering again why on earth he wanted to put a lock on that cupboard but feeling somehow sure that it was better not to ask.

With the correct tool the job went much better and was soon done; not the neatest job ever but it seemed secure and he was satisfied, thinking that he'd be able to offer Rory a safe storage place for his 'merchandise'. Rory'd definitely be pleased – probably he'd soon make him a partner in the enterprise – who knows? Sinking back on the lumpy old sofa he fell to daydreaming about how rich he'd be before long.

***

A tap at the back door made Lilian look up from her knitting – she had started to make a cot blanket from different patterned squares which she would back with some soft material. Siobhan bounced in closely followed by Maura; they were both dressed to go out and Maura had her shopping basket.

"Get your coat on, Lilian," said Maura. "I've made a barm brack and I thought we could go to visit Kitty Flaherty. She'll make us a cup of tea and you can meet her."

"That's a lovely idea – just give me a moment to finish my row and I'll be ready."

It took a little longer than finishing the row because Siobhan wanted to see what she was making, but soon she cleared up the knitting and fetched her coat. Being a smart, fitted style, Lilian's coat was having a bit of trouble meeting in the middle now but fortunately the day wasn't too cold.

In cheerful mood the two friends set off for the midwife's house a few streets away with little Siobhan alternately running ahead and holding both women's hands to swing.

"She's such a sweet little girl, Maura," said Lilian. "You must be really proud of her and she's such a sunny disposition."

"Yes, she's a happy little thing but she does have her moments,

I can tell you. And she's a bit spoiled by the other two, her being the youngest."

Mrs. Flaherty's door knocker was gleaming brass and very efficiently summoned the lady in question. Kitty's experienced eye quickly took in the situation of her visitors and ushered them into the warm kitchen.

"You must have known I've a kettle on the boil," said Kitty.

"Yes indeed, I thought you would have," replied Maura. She unwrapped the barm brack and introduced Lilian as the tea was prepared.

The cake was delicious with a little scrape of butter and they all enjoyed the tea while Kitty and Maura chatted about the children. Lilian found she readily warmed to the woman's open and pleasant manner.

After tea Kitty showed Lilian up to her bedroom, saying, "Let's just have a little look at how this babe's doing."

She checked her ankles for signs of swelling, her eyes for anaemia and then lifted her smock and warm jumper to listen to the baby's heart with a large, trumpet-like instrument.

"There's a good strong heartbeat there," she assured Lilian. "You're a strong, healthy girl so you'll be fine, to be sure. Just remember that you're eating for two now and make sure you have a bit of a rest every afternoon with your feet up."

"Yes, I usually do feel I need it lately," Lilian agreed.

"When the pains come regular you send someone along for me and I'll come straight away. I daresay Maura will help as well."

"Thank you very much," said Lilian, following Kitty back down the stairs. They said their goodbyes and were soon on their way back.

"What did you think of Kitty Flaherty?" asked Maura.

"She seems very nice and very reassuring but I'm a bit nervous, I must admit."

"That's only natural," replied her friend, "but Kitty's really experienced – everything'll be fine, you'll see."

"And I forgot to ask her about payment – what does she charge?"

"Not really a fixed amount – most people just give what they can afford. If I were you I'd put a little bit aside each week."

"Oh, I already do that, so that'll be O.K."

Siobhan, who had been running ahead, ran back and tugged at Lilian's hand just then.

"Lilian," she asked, "have you got a window in your tummy?"

"A window, whatever do you mean?"

"Well, Mrs. Flaherty said she wanted to look at the baby so I just wondered."

Maura and Lilian burst out laughing and Siobhan looked puzzled until Lilian explained: "She couldn't see the baby but she could hear him to check he's alright."

"Oh, can I hear him, then?"

"No, pet, you need a special thing to do that – like a sort of trumpet."

"Well, never mind," chirped the child, "I expect I'll hear him later on."

"Yes, I expect you will." Both girls laughed.

Chapter 19

A noise from downstairs woke Lilian with a jolt. She lay listening for a couple of minutes and heard more muffled movements and talking. Something to do with Desmond, then – he had lately taken to having visitors at dead of night. After a while the noises stopped and a soft click of the front door told her they'd gone. She soon drifted off to sleep still vaguely wondering why people came to see him only after dark.

Downstairs Desmond surveyed the newly delivered contraband with dismay. There were three crates and a couple of small barrels: how on earth was he going to conceal that lot? It was far too much for his padlocked cupboard and where it stood now would be clearly visible from the street. He could keep the curtains drawn but that would surely arouse suspicion in daylight. The best he could do was to pull the sofa round to hide some of it and made sure to go and see Rory about it in the morning.

The bar was almost empty when Desmond walked in, greeted by Rory in his usual affable landlord manner: "Top o' the morning to ee, my friend."

"Top o' the morning nothing," growled Desmond. "I need a word."

"A word, is it?" replied Rory, grinning and moving along the bar to draw a glass of stout. "I'm guessing you'll be needing a drink as well."

As soon as the glass was passed over Desmond took a deep draught, but before he could begin to voice his concerns to Rory, some new customers walked in and he had to wait.

Eventually Rory gestured to one of the booths in a corner so Desmond took his drink across and waited, feeling the stout calm some of the nerves and worries he'd come in with.

"What's your problem, then?" asked Rory, joining him in the booth with a sly look that said he knew full well what the problem was.

"You know I've no space to hide all that stuff," began Desmond.

"Keep your voice down," hissed Rory. "I thought you wanted to be part of the business."

"Yes, I do but---."

"Then you're gonna have to take some of the risk as well as the rewards. It'll just be a few days then I can get that moved on – now are you in or not?"

"Well, alright, but make sure it's only a few days."

"Good lad," smiled Rory, clapping him on the back as he rose to return behind the bar. "You won't be sorry – there'll be a good profit in that lot."

Much to Desmond's relief Rory turned up two nights later with a gig to load up the goods. After the job was done and the boxes carefully covered with some sacking, Desmond began to don his coat and scarf expecting to be driving the cargo to its destination but Rory interrupted him, saying, "Hold hard, lad, I'm gonna take this lot on but I've another wee task for you tonight. Actually, although it won't take you long – it's real important."

By the significant look and wink from the other man Desmond gathered that it would also be more lucrative so he wasn't going to argue.

"We can't talk about it here in the street," continued Rory, pulling a bottle from his pocket and raising it to indicate they should partake. Desmond willingly led him into the kitchen and took glasses from the dresser.

"What's the job, then?" asked Desmond as he sipped the liquor, feeling it warm his gut and raise his spirits.

"It's just a short delivery to this address," replied Rory, passing a scrap of paper and lifting an old canvas bag onto the table.

"What is it?"

"You don't need to know," came the answer in a slow, deliberate tone, "It's cash on delivery, so you collect the payment and I'll come and get it when I'm back in a day or so."

"Fair enough," said Desmond. Although it seemed a bit suspicious, he reckoned the cash would be worth it. "When would you like it done?"

"Tonight without fail and make sure no one sees you." Without another word he pocketed the bottle and left.

Desmond rubbed his hands over his face, drank some more whiskey and nervously regarded the bag. Like a child at Christmas he reached out and started to feel the shapes in the bag then quickly pulled his hands back at the thought of dangers in the bag. Eventually he could contain his curiosity no longer so carefully opened the drawstring of the bag and peered in; all he could see was some old fabric, probably curtains. What he saw when he gingerly moved aside set his heart pounding: there were two ugly handguns, as he had suspected.

Wrapping up the guns again and carefully retying the bag, he took a deep breath and gulped down the rest of the contents of the glass. He found himself in a total quandary: yes he could do with the money the job would earn, but he was almost afraid to pick the bag up, never mind deliver it; on the other hand, he didn't want to keep it in the house – that could surely be dangerous. He sat head in hands for some time but then pulled himself together, fetched his coat, hat and scarf and let himself out quietly, clutching the bag by its string, unable to bring himself to carry it on his shoulder.

Immediately outside the darkness enveloped him; it was moonless night with a cold, insistent drizzle. The conditions were good for it meant he met no one on the way; he walked close to the buildings, where there were some, and hedges when he left the town behind. Going along at a good pace, his heart began to pound and at one point thundered in his heart when a fox broke cover just in front of him.

There were no lights on in the farmhouse and no sign of life anywhere. Desmond knew better than to march up to the front door so he hung around near the house, sheltered by some hedges, and then made his way across towards the barn, wondering what to do next. A noise behind him made him turn and in an instant a hand was across his mouth and his arms pinned down. He was manhandled into the barn and pushed against one of the stalls – he had never been so frightened in all his life and it must have shown, for the first thing he heard as a lantern was lit was a throaty laugh and a gruff voice saying, "Keep your hair on, you'll come to no harm – just hand the goods over."

Sighing with relief, Desmond rapidly handed the bag over, blinking in the sudden lamplight. The lantern light revealed two men, probably only in their twenties but both with caps pulled well down and scarves over their faces. Although quaking inside, after all there were two of them, Desmond managed to retain his customary confidence and as they started to leave he caught hold of the nearest one and said, "Hold on, young man – I was told to collect cash on delivery."

"Well, fancy thinking we'd forget something like that," came the reply from the other man who reached into his pocket and handed over a handful of grubby notes. "We're going now," he said. "You wait a while before you leave and make sure you're not seen."

Desmond reckoned about ten minutes should be enough but the time passed slowly. He thought of counting the notes he'd stuffed into his pocket but decided better keep them out of sight.

After the first half-mile or so on the way back he began to relax and plan what he would do with his share of the cash. By the time he got home he'd had an idea and formed a plan he was really pleased with: he would 'borrow' some of the cash and use it to place bets at tomorrow's point-to-point race meeting. He had already had a great tip for a dead cert on one of the races so he reckoned he'd make a killing, pay back the stake and be well in profit.

Unfortunately, as so often happens, some of the horses he backed just didn't come up to scratch and when he left the field after the last race he was actually out-of-pocket – down a few punts.

Back at home he smoothed out the notes the best he could and put them in an envelope, awaiting Rory to collect. He didn't have long to wait as the publican called in on his way back from the trip upcountry. Lilian answered the door and called Desmond as she wasn't sure whether she should invite this stranger in.

Seeing who it was, Desmond had no choice but to invite him in and introduce his wife. Lilian merely smiled and answered politely, but Rory plastered on the Irish charm with twinkling eyes and extravagant compliments.

"We have a bit of business, my dear," interrupted Desmond, "so if you could excuse us."

"Of course," replied Lilian, actually really glad to retrieve her hand and retreat to the kitchen.

Without more ado Desmond handed over the envelope, assuring Rory that there'd been no trouble in carrying out the mission. Rory flicked through the notes and handed over a couple as the promised payment. It wasn't quite as much as Desmond had hoped but he didn't dare to query it.

At the pub later that night, Rory was busy behind the bar and didn't seem his usual ebullient self. Desmond thought he probably was playing it cool so that others wouldn't think too much about their business association, and anyway he had already made casual friends with some of the regulars, so he was in a relaxed and self-satisfied mood as he made his way home, weaving slightly due to one too many whiskies.

He hadn't gone far when he heard an odd whistle, sounding like some kind of signal and a moment later found himself hauled off his feet and into a nearby alley. He'd no chance to cry out before hard fists were in his face, his chest and his back. After long minutes of inflicted pain he fell to the ground where his assailants continued to rain well-aimed kicks on him before delivering the parting shot: "That'll teach you to double-cross Rory!" and ran off.

The adrenalin surging through his body enabled Desmond to drag himself to his feet where he leaned heavily against the wall while trying to make sense of what had just happened. Eventually he managed to clear his head enough to stagger out of the alley and get home. The house was all quiet as Lilian generally went to bed quite early.

Once indoors, with his heart still pounding nineteen to the dozen, he sank onto the lumpy old sofa in the parlour and began to take stock of his injuries. The surge of adrenalin had abated and he now began to shake violently with shock; his head was pounding and he discovered it hurt to breathe in too deeply. By some miracle the small bottle of rum in his jacket pocket had not broken so that became his solace until he mercifully fell into a deep sleep.

Lilian had heard her husband stumbling in the front door at around midnight and had not been surprised that he had remained downstairs for he often did so, attending to matters of business or just drinking.

In the morning she dressed quickly and went downstairs to

make a cup of tea; the range kept the kitchen reasonably warm and Lilian savoured her first cup of tea while daydreaming a little about taking the baby for a walk on a summer's day.

Dragging her thoughts back to the present, she poured another cup of tea to take through to Desmond. The sight of him, though, stopped her in her tracks: his face was covered in blood, one eye virtually closed, and a huge lump on his forehead.

"Whatever happened to you?" she gasped.

Desmond groaned a bit and winced as he pulled himself up a bit straighter in the chair.

"I had a fall," he muttered. "Is that tea? I can certainly do with that."

Even with Lilian's limited experience she knew for certain that he didn't get in that state just falling, but she didn't say anything, just fetched some warm water and a flannel so he could clean up.

Even though Desmond had a raging thirst he found drinking the tea very painful, due to his facial injuries and he only managed about half of it. There was no way he could contemplate eating and just groaned and shook his head slightly when Lilian asked if he wanted any breakfast. For the rest of the morning he dozed and nursed his aches and pains while wondering how Rory had known the money was short. By lunchtime another thirst had come upon him so he called Lilian and asked her to go to the off-licence for some brandy, justifying it as being needed for medicinal purposes.

Against her better judgement Lilian agreed but making the proviso that this would be the last time. She bought only a miniature, refusing to spend any more of her meagre housekeeping budget on drink.

Accepting the small bottle, Desmond just grunted and said, "That won't last long. Why didn't you get a bigger one?"

"I didn't have the money," replied Lilian.

"What do you do with all the money I give you, for goodness' sake?"

"Desmond, surely you can understand I have to eke out the housekeeping, because it's not really regular – it's three weeks since you gave me the last lot."

He ignored that, just lifting the bottle to his lips and taking a long swig.

***

After finishing the chores Lilian sat down in the kitchen for her afternoon rest; both Maura and the midwife had recommended she take a rest each day and she was certainly feeling a bit more tired now with her pregnancy advanced. She'd only been resting for a minute or two when she heard Desmond calling her name so reluctantly made her way to the parlour only to be greeted by a belligerent demand that she fetch him some more brandy. She sighed and shook her head but stood her ground.

"No, Desmond, I told you I haven't got the money. If you want more brandy you'll have to get it yourself."

"How can I when I'm injured?" he shouted.

As she turned to go he bellowed again, "Bitch!", and at the same instant the brandy bottle hurtled through the air at head height and smashed into the door only inches from her head.

Chapter 20

Lilian's pride would not let her show how frightened she was by such a violent reaction so she closed the door to the parlour very firmly and walked immediately through the kitchen, across the yard and into Maura's where she knocked once before entering her friend's kitchen. Maura was wiping down the kitchen table and looked up with a smile at once, but her smile froze when she saw how pale and shaken the other girl was.

"What's the matter, Lilian? What's happened? Is it the baby?" Without waiting for an answer she gently nudged the girl into the nearest chair, noting that she was shaking uncontrollably.

For several minutes Lilian could only shake her head while she tried to calm the thumping of her heart.

"He--- he threw a bottle at me, Maura," she gasped eventually.

"Did it hit you? Are you hurt?"

"No, I'm alright and the baby's alright," replied Lilian, protectively cradling her bump with both hands.

"Well, you've obviously had a nasty shock and the best thing for that is a nice cup of tea," said Maura, always practical.

When the tea was on the table and Lilian had got some of her colour back, Maura gently asked, "Has he been violent to you before?"

"Oh no, he never normally touches me – not that I want him to! He got angry because I refused to get him more brandy and obviously he's in pain – I think he's been beaten up."

Maura had seen Desmond about from time to time and noted that he looked a lot older than his wife and she'd also become aware of the nocturnal comings and goings next door. Clearly all was not well next door and it seemed that the girl had no idea what she'd got herself into.

"Did you only marry him because you were pregnant, Lilian?" asked Maura, leaning over to touch her friend's hand.

Lilian didn't reply for some minutes, then seemed to make a decision and sighed deeply before beginning: "My parents made me marry him because I was pregnant but the baby's not his. I hope we'll still be friends after I tell you what really happened."

"Of course we will, dear. It can't be that bad."

Lilian again paused for a while before telling her friend all about Michael, from the time they met in the bookshop, about the croquet game, about falling in love and the misery they felt when her parents refused to let them marry.

"They said we were too young and we should wait till after the war but he was going to be sent away and we were so in love!"

No further explanation was needed – in that sense it was not an uncommon wartime story.

"Do you know where he is now?" asked Maura gently.

"No, that's the worst part," whispered Lilian, unable to stop tears rolling down her cheeks. "I don't know what happened to him, I'll never see him again and he'll never see our baby."

Maura crossed the small space between them and put her arms around her friend, cradling and stroking her like a child until the sobbing subsided.

After a while Lilian pulled herself together and got up, saying, "I'm sorry. I've held you up long enough, I'm sure you've got lots to do, I'll be off back now."

"Will you be alright? Do you want me to come with you?" offered Maura.

"Oh no, thank you, but that would make him more angry – he doesn't even really like me talking to you. Thanks for the tea, Maura, see you later."

With that, Lilian was gone and Maura, glancing at the clock, realised she wouldn't have time now to make the cottage pie she had planned for the children's lunch, so instead she'd have to make some scrambled egg and toast. First she must collect Siobhan from her little friend's house down the road where she had gone to play earlier, so she grabbed her coat on the way to the front door, but just as she got there Sean and Kathleen were already coming in so she was able to send Sean to fetch his little sister and get on with the simple meal.

All three children chattered non-stop while the lunch was prepared and quickly demolished. So it wasn't until the older ones had gone back to school and she'd cleared up that Maura had a chance to reflect upon her morning.

She knew she'd been lucky with her Patrick: sure, they had words from time to time but they'd a love and respect for each other that never waned. Poor Lilian, on the other hand, seemed to be stuck with a thoughtless and arrogant man who hardly cared for her at all. This latest episode and the knowledge of his beating almost confirmed what Maura had suspected for a while, since she saw him in the company of some very unsavoury characters: namely that he was involved in something very dubious and possibly illegal. She didn't want to worry or upset Lilian any more, but she was beginning to think she should warn the girl for her own protection.

Back in the house Lilian listened for any movement from the front room and heard just muffled snores. Relieved that she wouldn't have to confront him, she set about warming some soup for her lunch and trying to carry on as normal. Normal meant taking a little rest after lunch which she did in the old armchair near the range; probably due to the earlier stress and shock she actually fell asleep for a while and was woken by Desmond calling her name.

She was tempted to pretend she hadn't heard but clearly she couldn't avoid him for ever, so taking a deep breath she pushed open the door and stepped over the broken glass.

"Did you call?"

"Yes, I'm really thirsty, do you think I could have a cup of tea?" he requested politely.

Lilian just nodded and returned to the kitchen to put the kettle on. No mention was made of the broken bottle, not then or later when Lilian bent down to sweep it up. He seemed to have a strange ability to block out incidents that he didn't want to remember.

Over the next few days Desmond's injuries began to heal and an uneasy peace settled between them in the house. As soon as he could move about a bit more freely he was off shuffling down to the nearest bar where he sat slumped over a pint, mulling over his position and his options.

Returning from a bit of shopping a day or two later, Lilian noticed a grubby-looking lad hanging about across the road and wondered why he wasn't in school – certainly looked of school age. As she put her key in the door he crossed over and approached her, saying, "Does Dezy Black live here, Missus?"

"Mr. Desmond Blackstock lives here," replied Lilian, shocking herself for a moment at how much she sounded like her mother.

"Yer! That's the fellar. Can you give him this please?"

With that, he thrust a crumpled envelope into her hand and shot off down the road. Lilian realised the reason for his rapid departure when she saw two members of the Garda turn the corner.

Desmond was back a bit later – he had stopped staying out until all hours – and Lilian handed him the envelope, saying, "A young lad left this for you. I don't know who it was – he ran off before I could ask him."

He looked at it suspiciously for a moment before ripping it open quite eagerly as though it might contain some pleasant surprise. After reading the contents his body language told quite another story: he went deathly pale, screwed up the paper and threw it in the range fire before leaving the room in silence. Lilian heard him banging about upstairs and a short time later he reappeared carrying an old rucksack.

"I'm going away for a while," he said.

"Where to?" asked Lilian, completely amazed.

"I don't know yet. There's some people I need to keep clear of.

Don't worry, they won't bother you."

With that, he was gone, leaving Lilian unsure whether to laugh or cry. What did he mean by 'a while'? Days, weeks, months, years? Probably he'd just overreacted to whatever the note said – probably he'd be back in a day or two like before. No need to fuss, she thought; she'd manage just fine!

Maura was in the habit of popping in most days, usually when Desmond had gone out – she seemed to have some sort of sixth sense about him – and sure enough she knocked and peered around the door a short time later.

"Is himself around?" she whispered.

"No, and I don't think he will be for a while."

Maura looked at her friend questioningly and the two women sat down while Lilian explained what had just happened.

"I'm sorry to say it, Lilian," sighed Maura, "but I'm not altogether surprised. He's been knocking around with some real rough types, you know. Anyway you'll have a few days' peace and quiet – think of it as a holiday; you'll be alright, won't you?"

"Hmm," replied Lilian uncertainly. "I suppose so."

Maura immediately picked up the girl's concern. "Has he left you enough money, Lilian?"

"He hasn't left me any. I've only got what's left from last week's housekeeping."

"Oh that man!" gasped Maura. "Don't worry, though, dear, we'll think of something."

An idea came to Maura that very evening when she sat down with her sewing box to repair yet again the holes young Sean regularly seemed to make in his pockets – why did boys always have to stuff their pockets with all sorts of objects?

She remembered Lilian had asked about borrowing a sewing machine and offered to help with repairs and alterations; she'd offered as a favour but people would pay good money for that sort of skill. As promised, Maura had asked a few people if they knew of a spare machine but without any luck; now she began to think about where else she could enquire. Before long, she hit upon the idea of putting cards in the local shop window and on the church noticeboard. She decided she'd do that tomorrow and not mention it to Lilian in the hope of being able to surprise her.

This she was able to do far sooner than she thought because only two days later the curate from the local church knocked on her door with the card in his hand and the good news that one of his parishioners, an elderly lady, was willing to pass on her sewing machine because severe arthritis meant she no longer enjoyed using it. They only needed to find a way to collect it, as apparently it was quite large.

"Oh that's wonderful news, thank you so much. I didn't dare to hope we'd get a result so soon. Won't you come in for a cup of tea, Father?"

"Well, I've another call to make on Mrs. Donovan, but I've never been known to refuse a cup of tea."

In the kitchen the young priest sat himself down at the table, making himself quickly at home while Maura busied herself with the tea.

"What are your plans with this here sewing machine, then?" he asked.

"Oh, it's not for me," replied Maura. "It's for my friend Lilian.

She lives next door and she's up against it at the moment, so I'm hoping that with her needlecraft skills she'll be able to make a bit of money to get by until….. Well, until her husband comes back."

Although they were not in the confessional, Maura felt confident that this information would go no further and in truth it probably wouldn't be long before it was common knowledge that he'd taken a break.

"If I can be of any help you've only to let me know," offered the young priest, sensing that there was a bit more to this than met the eye.

"Thank you, Father. I was just wondering if you knew anyone who could help us collect it?"

After thinking for a moment he came up with a suggestion: "I think Mrs. Milligan's sons would be able to help us and as a matter of fact he owes me a favour. When do you want to collect it?"

"How about tomorrow?"

"I think that can be arranged. Bring your friend down to the church in the morning."

Maura poured the tea before answering, then said, "I'd really like to surprise her so shall I not tell her till we bring it?"

"Oh," smiled the young priest. "Sure, I love a surprise – let's do that."

The big old treadle machine was loaded onto Mike Milligan's handcart the next day and before midday they knocked on Lilian's door. When she opened the door she saw a handsome young priest who cried, "Special delivery for Mrs. Lilian Blackstock!"

Maura was grinning behind him and on the pavement was a beautiful old sewing machine.

Chapter 21

Surprise was not the word: Lilian was astonished to see the smiling little deputation at her front door. Truth to be told, her thoughts had been going the same way as Maura's but she was several steps behind. Thus, as their eyes met, she realised and understood the reason behind the machine.

"Wherever did you get that?" she gasped.

"It belongs to an elderly lady who can't manage to use it anymore and she's happy for you to have it as long as you need it," answered Maura.

"Oh that's wonderful. I'll be able to do some repairs and alterations to help out if you think people will need it."

"Of course they do and maybe you can run up curtains and suchlike – people will be more than willing to pay for your skills."

"Where do you want it, then?" interrupted Mike, eager to be off about his own business.

"I think in the kitchen please. We might need to move the table over a bit, though."

Before long, it was installed near the window for good light and, although it made the kitchen rather crowded, it was after all the only really warm spot in the house.

Lilian thanked the men with a big smile, saying, "Father, before you leave please give me the lady's name and address so I can thank her properly."

"Ah, that's a kind thought – I will indeed," he replied taking the pencil and scrap of paper she handed him.

As the front door closed the two young women turned to each other, grinning, and fell into a great big hug.

"How did you do it so quickly, Maura?"

"It was easy – I just put cards in a few places asking for a machine. We can do exactly the same to advertise your services and I'll bet you'll have loads of clients in no time!"

Lilian suddenly got cold feet. "Hold on, I need to practise with it a bit first, especially because it's a treadle machine and I've never used one of those before."

"Come on, then, let's have a go – how difficult can it be?" Maura was not going to let her friend back down.

The old lady had also sent a box of threads, pins, spare needles and other haberdashery sundries, so Lilian chose a reel of thread and began to thread the machine; it was easy enough, quite similar to her mother's old machine and the bobbin was full so they were ready to go.

"Pass me a tea towel from the drawer, will you, Maura? We'll practise on that."

Seating herself at the machine, she spun the wheel and pushed down the treadle. The mechanism stalled and the thread broke! On the third try it caught and she got going for a few stitches but then lost the rhythm. By this time Lilian was getting disheartened but Maura got a fit of the giggles and soon Lilian was giggling, too.

Eventually she removed the tea towel and the tangled-up thread, saying, "I think I'll have to practise getting it going without threading first."

"Well, I'll wish you luck." Maura grinned. "I'd better be off now to sort out your first projects and get the kids' tea. See you tomorrow."

"Bye, Maura, and thank you."

She kept practising all evening, only stopping for a bit of toast for supper and by bedtime she was fairly happy she'd got the hang of it. All the time she'd been working on it she'd heard in her head her mother's voice saying, "If at first you don't succeed, try, try, try again." It was one of her favourite sayings and used to irritate Lilian, but how she missed that type of homespun advice now.

By morning, when Maura reappeared, Lilian had the machine threaded and was successful hemming a tea towel – just for practice.

"Well, now that's music to my ears," cried Maura. "I knew you could do it!"

Lilian was justifiably a little proud of herself so she carried on sewing, deftly turning the corner of the fabric and finishing off, holding the completed job up with a flourish.

Maura, as good as her word, had brought in some little repairs and alterations for Lilian to begin on and some blank postcards to prepare her adverts.

Maura took most of the cards the next day, leaving Lilian just to do the post office and the general store. Even before she had finished Maura's jobs her first customer was knocking on the door with quite a pile of good-quality gents' clothing that needed letting out: obviously the lady's husband had put on a little weight over the years and to have them let out would be much cheaper than to buy new.

To Lilian's surprise and delight her second customer was a face she recognised: "Good morning, Mrs. Blackstock?" enquired the young woman at the door.

"Oh hello," replied Lilian. "It's Aileen, isn't it?"

"Have we met?"

"Yes, sometime ago now – down by the stream. I'm Lilian."

"To be sure, I remember now and I can see why you were so interested in my Liam," said Aileen, glancing at Lilian's swollen belly.

"Yes, not long to go now," smiled Lilian. "Come on in, won't you?"

Aileen gathered her small son out of his pram and handed him straight to Lilian.

He was all smiles and not a bit perturbed at being handed to a perfect stranger. His mother then fished about in the bottom of the pram for a parcel which contained one of her dresses. Lilian pulled the cushions off the armchair and sat Liam among them in case he toppled over, before turning back to Aileen. As tempting as it was to play with the baby, she must be businesslike first of all.

Aileen shook the dress out of the parcel and held it up against her. "I was wondering if you could alter this, Lilian, 'cos altho' I like the fabric, it's a bit old-fashioned, don't you think?"

"Well, you're right, it is a lovely fabric and it could look really nice if we take the skirt off, put in some darts for shape and shorten it a bit. What do you think?" As she spoke, Lilian had illustrated what she meant, coaxing the fabric into the shape she envisaged.

"That sounds perfect – I'm sure it'll look marvellous. How long will it take?"

"I need to finish the job I've got on at the moment before I get on to it, but probably I could get it done by the end of the week."

"Oh that'd be fine. Do I need to come for a fitting or anything?"

"We can pretty well do that now, I think, but shall we have a cup of tea first?"

"I'll do it, shall I?" offered Aileen. "I can see you're itching to have a cuddle with himself."

"How could you tell?" Lilian smiled and nodded, holding her arms to the cooing baby.

As they chatted over their tea Lilian explained that Desmond had got into a bit of trouble and had to go away for a while but she did not mention about him being beaten up or anything about him not being the baby's father.

"I'm doing the sewing to make ends meet until he comes back," she said.

When Aileen said, "Surely he'll want to be back in time for the baby's arrival," Lilian just replied, "I don't think he's bothered," and changed the subject.

No sooner had Aileen and Liam gone than there was another knock at the door which turned out to be Father Dermot enquiring about how she was getting on with the sewing machine. Since he had been instrumental in obtaining the machine, Lilian thought it only polite to ask him in and show him what she was doing. He was most interested and she ended up making another pot of tea.

Lilian found the young priest very easy to talk to and they chatted for quite some time – she couldn't help thinking he didn't really seem like a priest at all. He was very appreciative that she had made the effort to personally thank the elderly donor of the machine, taking with her a little posy of flowers, even though they were only wild flowers from the hedgerow.

On the appointed day Aileen returned to collect her restyled dress and was delighted with it. She didn't have Liam with her this time, saying her sister-in-law had him for the afternoon. She apparently lived over near the big house.

Aileen was thrilled with the results of Lilian's work. She could hardly believe she'd made it look so much more fashionable. She didn't stay as long on this visit as she'd to get back to feed Liam, but left promising to return in a day or two and to tell her sister-in-law and all her friends about Lilian's skills.

"I'm sure lots of them will have work for you," she assured her friend.

It was more than a week before Aileen returned and, although she was busy, Lilian was a bit disappointed that she'd left it longer than she said. She was glad to see Aileen, though, and immediately took Liam from her, bouncing and petting him. Aileen had brought some home-made scones which were very welcome with a nice pot of tea but, oddly, their conversation seemed forced and stilted even with Liam claiming much of their attention. After an awkwardly silent gap of a few minutes Aileen broached the subject that had been bothering her: "I hope I'm not speaking out of turn, Lilian, but how much do you know of your husband's background?"

"What do you mean?" asked Lilian, immediately suspicious.

"I only ask because my sister-in-law told me she doesn't think you'll get any work from her neighbourhood because he's got a bad reputation over there."

Lilian made no reply so she went on. "Apparently he conned two old ladies out of their life savings by getting them to invest in his non-existent company. And one of them became so distraught that she took her own life."

Lilian sighed deeply and bowed her head.

Thinking she was crying, Aileen reached out to comfort her, but she was dry-eyed and merely said, "That explains his father's attitude when we called on him."

As this new blow sank in, Lilian put her head in her hands and did begin to weep, saying softly, "I don't know what I'm going to do if this doesn't work, Aileen. I don't know when he's coming back or if he's coming back and I've only got what I can earn to live on."

Handing her friend a clean hankie, Aileen said, "Don't cry, Lilian. Come on – we'll think of something. I know, let's change your cards and make new ones using your maiden name – that'll solve the problem and while he's not here he won't know." Lilian sighed and brightened a bit.

"I suppose we can try that. Goodness, I never knew what I was getting into coming here."

Chapter 22

Maura cheerfully helped Lilian to retrieve, change and replace her cards, though of course she had to explain the reason she felt it necessary. Her friend nodded while she told the saga but didn't really seem surprised. Straight away she got started on the task, saying that she thought it should say:

Lilian Woodridge – Dressmaking and Alterations – 6 The Terrace – Bramwell

Whether it was the new name or the kind people of the area realising that she was properly up against it, with her husband away indefinitely, business certainly improved quite a bit. A surprising flurry of work came from the church due to the fact that it would soon be May when the children usually take their first Holy Communion. Lilian had no idea that on that occasion little girls are dressed like princesses, all in white and often with a veil. Few families could afford new dresses but borrowed from cousins or friends, so they would often need altering to fit or some new trimming to freshen them up.

It was just such a job that Lilian was working on when Siobhan appeared at the door clutching her rather disreputable favourite teddy bear.

"Hello, Lilian. What are you making?"

Siobhan had a tendency to want to touch the fabrics Lilian worked on, so she quickly warned: "Don't touch, Siobhan, unless your hands are clean."

The little girl held her hands out to inspect them and pulled a face. "I'd better wash them right now," she offered, putting the teddy down and going over to the sink.

"That's a good girl," smiled Lilian, "then I'll show you – it's a First Communion dress."

She'd just finished putting a little lace collar onto the dress and it had a pale blue velvet sash.

"Oh it's beautiful!" cried Siobhan when Lilian held it up to show her. "I wish I had a dress like that."

"I expect you will, Siobhan, when you're older."

"How old do you have to be?"

"About eight or nine, I think."

"That's ages," sighed Siobhan, wistfully stroking the soft velvet. She thought for a few moments, then said, "My teddy's eight or nine – I know he is because Sean had him before me – so he's old enough."

Lilian smiled at the wheedling tone that had entered the child's voice.

"I don't think teddies really have First Communion dresses, poppet, but I could make one for one of your dollies if you like."

"Would you?" Siobhan's face lit up. "I'll go and fetch Marina straight away!"

Truth to be told, Marina was only slightly less disreputable than the teddy, having had her face washed in the bath before now and her hair brushed none too gently, but Siobhan loved her and was thrilled at the prospect of a new dress for her. Lilian said she'd keep her overnight and take good care of her while she was having her new dress fitted and Siobhan went back home to tea in a fever of anticipation.

Knowing that the little girl would be expecting some miracle of transformation by the morning, Lilian worked later than usual with leftover scraps of fabric and lace to produce a sweet little frock, and managed to concoct a simple veil to hide the doll's scraggy hair. Pleased with her efforts, she dressed Marina in her new finery and sat her on the table ready for Siobhan next morning and was reminded how, in happier times, her mother had carried out just such labours of love for her.

She'd just cleared away and put on some soup to heat for supper when there came a knock at the door. It wasn't common but not unknown for customers to call in the early evening, so Lilian pasted a professional smile on her face and opened up. It was Father Dermot who'd already called by quite often for a cup of tea and a chat while subtly trying to persuade her to attend church. Not wanting to be rude, she asked him in and offered to make tea as usual.

"No, no, my dear," he replied. "Thank you but I just had tea with Mrs. Donnelly down the road."

Seeing the prettily dressed little doll on the table, he picked her up admiringly and asked, "Is this for your new little babe?"

"Oh no," laughed Lilian. "She's for Siobhan, Maura's little girl

– she's such a little darling! Oh hark at me – I sound more Irish than you!"

For some reason that wiped the smile from his face and now, abandoning subtlety, asked directly, "When will I see you at church, then, Lilian?"

Although a bit surprised by his bluntness, Lilian, who had been thinking about church and in some ways missing the routine of home, answered: "I thought I might come on Sunday with Maura actually – I'm sure she wouldn't mind." She didn't add that she supposed it couldn't be too much different from what she was used to, although Agnes used to say that Catholics were a 'funny lot' in spite of not actually knowing any.

"Well, now, that'll be a grand idea. Sure we'll all be glad to see you." Then he did that odd thing of glancing up to Heaven and crossing himself. Lilian smiled faintly but silently vowed that she wouldn't be copying that.

Siobhan was delighted with Marina's new dress and managed to keep it clean for quite a few days while Lilian did her best to complete all her outstanding work, knowing that she wouldn't be able to work for at least a few weeks after the birth. With Maura's approval she hadn't really done a fixed tariff for services but nobody took advantage, with the result that cash was often supplemented by some cheese or eggs or fresh vegetables as payment.

On Sunday morning Lilian put on her coat and the only hat she had with her – her 'going away' hat – and waited by the window until Maura and the children emerged ready for church. On the way she and Maura chatted while Siobhan ran on ahead and the older children rather lagged behind. On entering the lovely old church, Lilian recognised several of her customers and was greeted by nods and smiles which gave her a warm feeling of beginning to belong to this community.

The service itself was a bit difficult to follow, being mostly in Latin, so she didn't know any of the responses but sitting beside Maura she was able to take her lead and stand up, sit down or pray at the right times. Father Dermot took the service – it was strange to see him looking so distant in his ecclesiastical robes when she was more used to him casually drinking tea in her kitchen. The sermon or homily, as it was called, was about loving your fellow man and thankfully was not too long.

Emerging into the pleasant early spring sunshine, the first person they met was Kitty Flaherty who smiled approvingly at Lilian, saying, "I can see you're doing all the right things – you're absolutely blooming, my dear!" What Lilian didn't see as they left was a nod and a wink to Maura, indicating that the midwife's instinct foretold the birth to be imminent.

Sure enough, in the middle of the night, Lilian was woken by an unfamiliar hard squeeze in her abdomen; it didn't last long and she tried to get back to sleep but after a while it happened again and soon there was no mistaking that her baby was on the way. The plan was to call Maura as soon as something happened but since it was still dark she pulled on her dressing gown and went downstairs to make a cup of tea, deciding to wait as long as she could before calling her friend. To her surprise she managed to doze a bit in the kitchen chair before being woken by a much more definite pain that lasted too long. It was light by now and she made her way to the back door, hoping she'd be able to make Maura hear. Her luck was in because she could already hear Siobhan out in the yard chattering to one of her dolls.

"Siobhan," she called, "will you get Mummy for me please?"

Maura was there in a minute and took one look at her before taking charge.

"Let's get you upstairs right away, then I'll send Sean to fetch Kitty Flaherty."

The next few hours were a bit of a blur but oh how glad she was of Maura's support and Kitty's professionalism.

At last it was all over! She'd a beautiful baby girl and she called her Michelle.

The baby didn't feed well and didn't sleep well; everyone had advice – Kitty, Maura and Aileen – but no one understood her exhaustion and her fear that her baby wasn't thriving. So it was that Dermot found her weeping at the kitchen table while Michelle howled in her makeshift cot.

Without missing a beat he swept up the screaming infant and put a strong arm around Lilian, pulling her in close until her sobbing subsided. Somehow his calm strength was just the comfort she needed. It wasn't long before Lilian recovered enough to feed the baby while the young priest tidied round in the kitchen and made a snack of sorts. He didn't stay long, abandoning his intended mission of suggesting a date for Michelle's baptism; instead he made a few calls to rally a support group. This soon meant that almost every day someone arrived with a nourishing soup, a custard, a milk pudding, or to give a hand with the washing.

Chapter 23

The christening was to be on Sunday directly after the morning service. All the arrangements had been made by Father Dermot who was secretly rather pleased that he'd persuaded Lilian and so was gaining a new member of his flock. For her part, Lilian knew that if she'd still been in Stonebury or Market Stamford the christening would be a big event with a special white christening robe, a christening cake and a party afterwards, probably with sherry to 'wet the baby's head'; this baptism would be very low-key in comparison.

After most of the congregation had left, a little group gathered around the ancient carved font at the back of the church. Maura and Aileen were to be godmothers and Father Dermot to stand as godfather. A few older ladies stayed behind to watch as well and murmur approval when Michelle screamed loudly as the priest poured cold water over her head and into the font: apparently it was a good sign if the child cried at that point.

As soon as it was over, Lilian wrapped her shawl tightly around Michelle and started to hurry home, wanting to get her baby properly warm and dry in case she would catch a cold. She hadn't got very far when she heard footsteps and turned to see Dermot running to catch her up. He was smiling and as soon as he got to her, he handed her a small package.

"It's just a little gift for Michelle to welcome her to the church."

It was a small prayer book, very prettily decorated and obviously quite special. Lilian was touched at his thoughtfulness and thanked him with tears in her eyes. They walked on together as Lilian explained the reason she wanted to get home quickly.

Arriving at home, Lilian felt obliged to ask him in for a cup of tea in view of his kindness. Just inside the front door she almost fell over a small suitcase and sure enough there was Desmond, sitting at the kitchen table with a bottle of beer, looking quite like his old self.

"Oh Desmond, you're back!" she exclaimed.

"So it would seem, my dear," murmured her errant husband, sourly taking in the babe in her arms and the handsome young priest behind her.

"And who have we here?" he continued.

His voice held a familiar note of menace, causing Lilian to hesitate a moment before lifting the baby towards him and saying, "She's just been christened."

"Well, well, well and she's a pretty little thing."

Much to Lilian's surprise his voice softened at the sight of Michelle: he smiled and gently touched her cheek. Turning to Dermot, he asked, "I presume you organised that, did you? …..Father….."

"Dermot," supplied the young priest, extending a hand to be shaken.

"Well, thank you for that," replied Desmond, rising and ignoring the proffered hand. "I'm sure you have God's business to be getting on with."

Dermot found himself ushered out of the door cordially but, it had to be said, quite rapidly.

As soon as the door was closed Desmond turned to Lilian, the veneer of charm gone, and almost shouted, "I told you I didn't want busybodies in this house! Is that clear?!"

The tone and volume of his speech frightened Michelle, who began to howl first from fright and then from hunger.

Lilian couldn't help but protest. "Desmond, he really helped me a lot. You were away – I had no money – what was I supposed to do?"

He took another swig of beer before muttering: "Behave yourself for once."

By now, Lilian was also in tears so she picked up the squalling baby, saying, "I have to feed her," and took her upstairs.

As she suckled the baby whilst rocking her she calmed down and began to reflect on how different Desmond was in some situations. He could charm – for sure he'd charmed her parents – and it was almost like he was two people in the same skin.

Michelle was very sleepy – almost fell asleep during her feed. Getting christened is obviously very tiring; consequently she went straight away to sleep in her makeshift cot without the usual grizzling that she was prone to do in the evening.

Before going downstairs Lilian stopped a few minutes to gaze and wonder at this perfect creature before squaring her shoulders to return to the kitchen. Her misgivings were justified for she had hardly stepped through the door before Desmond growled, "What's THAT doing here!?" nodding his head to indicate the sewing machine.

"I use it to do dressmaking and alterations for people."

"What for?"

"For money of course. I had to live, didn't I? When you went off I had almost no money. What was I supposed to do?"

Desmond looked quite taken aback but, not ready to climb down, he snarled. "Where did it come from?"

"Father Dermot got it for me …."

She hadn't finished explaining about the elderly lady when Desmond exploded: "Father Dermot! I thought so! Have you no shame, woman? Crawling to a priest!"

Calmly and in an ice-cold voice, Lilian replied, "I had no choice."

"Well, it stops now. I'm back now and I do the providing." So saying, he threw a handful of notes and coins onto the table before flouncing out and calling back, "Make sure there's some decent food on the table when I get back!"

The front door slammed and Lilian sat down at the table to count the money. She was amazed at how calm she felt, but also quite determined that she would carry on with the little business she had built up, whatever he said.

There was quite a bit of money – whatever he'd been doing while he was away must have been lucrative. If the shops were open she could stock up the larder but of course there's nothing open on a Sunday evening. Ah well, thought Lilian, there's some mince and potatoes so it'll have to be cottage pie. She set to and put the meal together, making it as tasty as she could with plenty of seasoning. It was soon in the oven on a low heat to heat through and crisp up the top.

Soon Lilian began to feel really hungry and the cottage pie smelled good. It was long after her usual suppertime so she decided to dish up the meal and keep Desmond's warm on a plate.

Unsurprisingly he didn't return while the food was still fresh and appetising; he didn't even return when it was dried up and inedible. Lilian had long gone to bed when she heard the latch on the door and his stumbling steps. She sighed and tried to get back to sleep – clearly things were going to be much the same.

Some days in the following weeks Desmond did seem to be making an effort to stay sober and be pleasant. He showed real affection for the baby, often playing with her or bringing home some little trinket.

Other times he would be out for hours on end and the strange nocturnal comings and goings began again. Trouble was, whereas before Michelle was born, if he returned the worse for wear he'd crash out on the sofa, but now he frequently made it upstairs and into Lilian's bed.

Because of the fuss Desmond had made about the sewing machine Lilian had continued to do her dressmaking, but covertly when he was out, and always made sure to clear away all the evidence of fabric or threads. Unfortunately things came to a head one evening when she stayed up late to finish an order and he returned unexpectedly. He was whistling when he opened the door but as soon as he set eyes on her machine his face darkened like thunder and he roared, "I thought I told you to get rid of that thing?!"

"Desmond, I can't, I need it for my work and it's not in the way!" she cried.

His anger filled the room as he grabbed her by the arm and seethed: "You get rid of it or I will. Do you understand?"

"Alright, alright – I will," sighed Lilian, pulling her arm out of his grasp and rubbing it where a red weal had formed. "I'll do it in the morning."

On his way out next morning Desmond ominously muttered, "That'd better not be here when I get back."

All night, Lilian had been miserable about having to return her now-beloved sewing machine and wondered about the best way to arrange for its return. As soon as Michelle went down for her nap Lilian popped next door to see Maura and ask how to get in touch with Mike Milligan to borrow his handcart.

Scrubbing brush in hand, Maura was rubbing away at grubby clothes on the washboard but as soon as she saw Lilian she grinned and dried her hands, saying, "Oh, I'm glad to see you, Lilian. I need a rest from this. I don't know how my kids get their clothes so dirty."

Lilian smiled weakly and sat down at the kitchen table.

"I've come to ask a favour, Maura."

"Ask away!"

"I wondered if I could borrow Mr. Milligan's cart again because I've got to get rid of the sewing machine. Do you know how to get in touch with him?"

Maura looked across at her in amazement. "Why on earth are you getting rid of it? I thought you loved it."

"I do and I really don't want to get rid of it, but Desmond says I must – he doesn't like it in the house and he doesn't like me doing the sewing."

Maura turned to put the kettle back on the range – her answer to most things – and then sat down opposite her friend.

"Look, Lilian, do you still want to carry on with the dressmaking?"

"Yes, of course I do. I love doing it and the money's really useful. Now Desmond's back he's given me some money, but to be honest, I don't know how long that will last. But he's absolutely adamant."

Maura said nothing, not wanting to voice her opinion of the other girl's husband but picked up the ever-ready teapot and proceeded to pour in hot water.

"Can you help me, then, Maura?" asked Lilian.

"Yes, I can, but let's have a think first. How about if I look after the machine and you can use it whenever you want to?"

Lilian gasped with delight at such a kind offer. "That's a wonderful, idea Maura, but have you enough room?"

Maura thought for a moment, wondering if she had been a bit too hasty but then had an idea. "I reckon I can move things about a bit in the front room and you could do it there. We don't actually use it very often – we're mainly in here."

With tears in her eyes at the kindness of her good friend, Lilian jumped up to hug and thank her. "I need to pop back and check on Michelle and then – well – do you think the two of us can get it in here before he comes back?"

"It's pretty heavy, isn't it? Tell you what, I'll call Sean to give us a hand – he's quite strong. Together we'll manage."

Chapter 24

Lilian was concerned that in her innocence Siobhan might let the cat out of the bag that the sewing machine had gone next door, but she needn't have worried because the child seemed to have a sixth sense that she shouldn't be there when Desmond was at home; it was quite uncanny, the number of times, almost in the middle of a conversation or a game, that she'd suddenly say, "I'll go now," and would disappear out of the back door as the man of the house came in through the front door.

He had made no comment about the disappearance of the machine, seeming to take it for granted that his word was law. Occasionally he remarked that Lilian seemed to be spending a lot of time next door, but she always made some excuse about looking after the children or sharing a recipe or just having a chat. His response was usually along the lines of "Huh, you women! Don't know what you find to talk about all the time!"

Just as before, Desmond was out most of the time which Lilian was quite glad about but at least the money he erratically produced covered the rent and most of the bills. How different their financial position was from what she'd been brought up to and surely from what her parents had expected. Back at home, Edward had always drawn the same amount from his salary at the end of the week and bought it home to Agnes, where they would sort it into several old tobacco tins that were kept in the bureau to make sure there was always enough for their bills and regular expenses. Lilian found their hand-to-mouth existence quite a strain and if she hadn't had her little income from the dressmaking she would have found it a struggle to manage.

As the soft days of the Irish summer progressed, Aileen and Lilian often met up to take a walk together and give the babes an airing. Their favourite walk was down to the little stream off the main street where the girls had first met some months ago. Even the drizzly rain that was so much a feature of the climate here didn't stop them meeting and chatting to exchange news of their brilliant offspring's latest achievements. Some of the little gardens they passed reminded Lilian of the neat little plots in her home town before their owners had been obliged to grub up well-loved roses and lush perennials to plant cabbages and beans instead. Her favourite garden along the way they usually walked was only small but it had beautiful lilac tree in the corner and a riotous bed of mixed lupins and larkspur, as well as roses around the door; for some reason it reminded Lilian of Muriel's garden, although in truth it was much more artistically planted. As they passed one day she started to talk to Aileen about her friend back in England and reminiscing about the fun they used to have together.

"I know I should write to her and let her know my address but it was hard at the beginning here and lately I've been so busy but

I really will make the effort!" she promised herself.

The arrangement the two girls had was always to meet on the corner near this particular garden, as it was convenient for both of them. One pleasant sunny morning Lilian was a bit later than usual getting to their meeting point because Michelle had been a bit fractious over her feed and managed to be sick on the clean dress she'd put her in. Being late, she expected Aileen to be already there but the road was quite empty. It was no hardship to wait a while, rocking the old pram (borrowed from Maura) to lull the baby and enjoy the fresh air. She waited quite a long time, however, and began to think her friend wasn't going to show.

Just as she was about to give up and continue her walk alone, Aileen came hurrying round the corner.

"Sorry I'm late, Lilian. I thought you might have gone."

"Hello, Aileen, I was just about to go on but never mind, I was a bit late myself today – little 'Miss' decided to be sick just after I got her ready."

Aileen just nodded and without looking at her friend or the baby set off down the road towards the stream without really waiting for Lilian. Catching her up, Lilian caught a glimpse of red eyes and a set to her lips that wasn't anything like her usual sunny expression. Neither girl spoke until they reached the bench where it was their habit to sit and chat a while. Lilian at first tried to make light conversation about the weather and successfully made little Liam laugh by tickling and teasing him with a toy, but his mama remained quiet and withdrawn. Being herself a very private person, Lilian was loath to intrude if her friend didn't want to talk but as she turned back from playing with the little lad Aileen was gazing across the hills with tears pouring down her face.

"What's the matter, Aileen?"

Lilian leaned towards her friend and took her hands in her own.

After a few moments she replied, "It's Donal."

Lilian had never met Aileen's husband but from the way she always spoke about him it was clear they had a happy, loving relationship. Thinking that maybe they'd had a row, she asked, "What's he done?"

Aileen took a deep breath, sighed it out and began. "He's going to England to enlist! He wants to fight the Nazis and I've begged him not to go but he won't listen; it's not like he has to go – it's different for the men who have to go, but Ireland's not in the war."

"Anyone who goes to fight that awful man is brave and honourable, Aileen, just like Michelle's father."

"Oh, I know, Lilian, but I'm sure he's going to be killed and I just don't know what I'd do. I want Liam to grow up with a daddy." Saying this, she leaned over and picked the little lad up from his pram for comfort really but seeing his mama looking so sad Liam's lips began to quiver as well.

Not wanting a crying baby on her hands as well, Lilian lifted him from her and jiggled him on her knee. "Come on now, Aileen, dry your eyes and think with your head, not your heart: number one – he'll probably be fine; number two – he's doing it for you and Liam, isn't he!? So Liam can grow up in a free and safe world; and number three – if he doesn't go because of you, he may come to blame himself and you for failing to do his duty."

Lilian wasn't sure where this little speech had come from but she was rather proud of it and it certainly did the trick. Aileen soon bucked up and began to feel more positive.

Lilian's earlier mention of Michael had encouraged Aileen to ask about him on the way back home and Lilian found it wasn't now quite so painful to talk about him and their time together: some of the sharp edges of her grief had worn off so that her overwhelming feeling was pride at having known and loved him.

After the girls parted, Lilian turned into her road just in time to see Desmond leaving the house, looking slightly furtive and carrying his rucksack that appeared to be heavy. He hadn't said anything about going away again but then he didn't say much at all about his 'business', as he called it. At any rate if he's going to be out this afternoon, thought Lilian, I can put Michelle down for a nap and get on with some needlework – she'd promised one lady her curtains by the end of the week. Her husband didn't appear to suspect that she was still running her little business, though he had commented once or twice that she seemed to spend an awful lot of time next door. Since then she tried to do it mostly when he was out and often delivered finished items herself to avoid customers coming to the house. It was just as well she did have her own income because financial support from Desmond continued to be erratic in the extreme: sometimes he'd come home in expansive mood and throw a handful of notes onto the kitchen table, looking very pleased with himself and had even been known to bring home little gifts for the baby. Other times he'd sourly demand what was left of the housekeeping and stamp around looking in drawers and clothes for spare coins.

Lilian was careful to keep the money she earned separate from her housekeeping and it was just as well she did, because on more than one occasion she needed to dip into it for things that Michelle needed.

On her way back from delivering the curtains Lilian met Maura, basket over her arm and with Siobhan skipping along beside her, on the way to the shops. "Hello, Lilian, I'm glad I've seen you – don't think I'm prying but I'm wondering what your man is up to indoors. He's been banging about in there fit to come through the wall at one point!"

"Oh dear, I hope he's not been drinking so early but thanks for the warning."

"Just you take care, my love."

They chatted a while longer as Siobhan peered into the pram, tickling Michelle to make her giggle.

When she opened the front door the house was quiet and she breathed a sigh of relief until she saw the state of the kitchen: it looked as if someone had ransacked it – drawers all thrown open and pots and pans all over the place. Nothing appeared to be broken, though, so she set to work tidying it after sitting Michelle safely in the corner. She'd not got very far when Desmond came stomping down the stairs and threw the kitchen door open.

"What's this?!" he roared, waving Michelle's birth certificate close to her face.

Oh no, thought Lilian, if he's found that he's also found the little nest egg put aside for emergencies.

"You can see what it is," she replied, struggling to remain calm because she could see he was furious about something.

"You even had to put your soldier boy down on here, didn't you? It's like you're proud of what you did."

"It's only right to put her real father's name down," answered Lilian, "and please stop shouting: you'll make her cry."

"Only right?!" he shouted even louder. "I suppose that mealy-mouthed priest put you up to it, did he?"

"No, he didn't and he's not mealy-mouthed, he's a good man and he helped me a lot."

"Oh, I bet he did and helped himself no doubt to get his feet under the table while I was away."

At that point Michelle did take fright and started to wail loudly so Lilian turned to pick her up and when she turned back he was gone – slamming both doors loudly behind him.

Chapter 25

For some weeks Michelle had been pulling herself up and taking a few tottering steps, already showing herself to be an inquisitive little soul, into everything, so Lilian was kept busy just keeping tabs on her.

She loved to find something she could pick up and present to her mother like a prize or a gift; this game was fun for both of them and helpful for language development. Just after breakfast one morning Lilian heard the letter box click and Michelle was off to pick up the letter and bring it to the kitchen.

"Thank you, poppet. Well, somebody's sent us a letter." It was addressed to Lilian and postmarked England. Lilian's immediate thought, with a glow of pleasure, was that Maureen had replied to the letter she'd eventually sent quite a while ago, but it wasn't Maureen's handwriting.

Puzzling for a moment, she sat down at the kitchen table with Michelle on her lap to read it. It was a sad little note from Maureen's mother explaining that her daughter had gone to London to meet her fiancé Jack and they'd been in a club dancing when an air raid was on. There was a direct hit and they were both killed.

Lilian read it over and over, struggling to come to terms with such awful news and feeling numb from the shock.

After a short while Siobhan peeped around the door – she was a frequent visitor, loving to play with the baby and not yet at school. A little girl seemingly wise beyond her years, she saw straight away that something was wrong so she called through the fence for her ma to come quickly.

Maura was there like a shot, fearing that something may have happened to the baby.

"What's wrong, Lilian?" she asked, seeing the girl gazing into space. With a sigh of relief she saw Michelle happily playing on the floor as she approached her friend.

Lilian handed her the note, saying softly, "She loved to dance, Maura."

"Oh Lilian, that was your friend you told me about."

"Yes, we were at school together. She was so full of life and Jack was in Michael's unit, so…" Then the tears came and Lilian struggled to go on speaking. "So he might have known what happened to him. Don't you see? If Jack was alive maybe he was, too, and now I'll never know."

Lilian's tears became racking sobs and Maura whispered to Siobhan to take Michelle out into the yard before cradling her friend until she calmed down.

"It's no good thinking about that, dear. You didn't know, so you couldn't do anything."

"If only I'd written to her earlier," she whispered, sighing deeply.

"Come on, I'll make a pot of tea," smiled Maura. "That always helps."

"Yes," said Lilian, pulling herself together. "I'm sorry, it must have been the shock of the news in the letter."

Maura called the girls in and brewed the tea, exclaiming at how well Michelle was walking now and giving her a little cuddle. She was such a sweet little thing, a great favourite with everyone who knew her.

No sooner had they finished their first cup of tea than there was a loud rap at the front door. The two women looked at each other, both a bit shocked at the imperious nature of the knock.

"Who on earth is that? I wonder. Only one way to find out," said Lilian, getting up to go to the door, closely followed by Michelle.

Lilian gasped with surprise to see two officers of the Garda standing at the door.

"Yes," she stuttered, "can I help you?"

The two men looked her up and down, no doubt taking in her red eyes from weeping earlier.

"Nothing to worry about, madam," one replied.

"Just some help with our enquiries," continued the other.

"Does a Mr. Desmond Blackstock reside here at all?" asked the first one.

They were like some sort of weird double act.

"Yes, but he's out," replied Lilian.

"When will he be back?" the double act continued.

"I really don't know but I'll tell him that you called." Lilian was beginning to feel anxious now as the two men stepped closer and tried to peer over her shoulder. At that moment Michelle appeared beside her mother, Maura must have put her down.

One of the men bent down and spoke to the child: "We've

come to see your daddy."

They both watched the little girl closely, clearly hoping she would give something away. Lilian picked her daughter up, angry at the way they were trying to trick a child.

"I told you he is not here!"

Just then came the sound of a door banging within the house.

"He's trying to get away round the back," cried one, dashing away to get round the back of the terrace.

"That was just my next-door neighbour," protested Lilian.

"Hmmm, a likely story." The Garda officer who'd spoken first peered around her again and appeared to consider pushing his way in, but then thought better of it and backed off. The one who'd run around the back re-emerged further up the street shaking his head and the other sauntered off to join him, saying, "We'll be back, Missus."

As Lilian closed the door she realised her heart was thumping madly and she was shaking: why? She hadn't done anything wrong, and whatever they might think Desmond had done she knew nothing about. The tea on the kitchen table had gone cold and Maura hadn't even finished hers – she must have decided she really didn't want to get involved.

Not wanting to waste the tea, Lilian boiled up some water to freshen up the pot but she ended up pouring most of it away with a heavy heart at the bad news she'd received today. What else can happen? she wondered, having her mother's old superstition that bad news always comes in threes.

Several hours later while Michelle was taking her afternoon nap, Desmond returned and plonked down a heavy bag, saying,

"I could murder a brew and what is there to eat?"

"Before that," replied Lilian, "I'd better tell you that the Garda were here asking for you."

"What!?" exclaimed Desmond. "What did they want? What did you tell them?"

"I told them you were out of course. They just said they wanted help with their enquiries."

"You stupid woman: why didn't you say I'd gone away or something? You didn't let them in, did you?"

"No, I didn't, but what did they want? Desmond, what have you done?"

"Nothing that you need to worry about but this means I'll have to lie low for a while. Damn and blast it," he muttered, picking up the bag he had just dropped and leaving by the back door. Pausing at the back gate he called back in a sort of strange whisper, "I'll be back in a few weeks. If they come back don't tell them anything!"

Then he was gone, leaving Lilian absolutely aghast. How could he just up and leave like that? At least this time she had some money because he had handed some over a few days ago, saying he'd had a bit of luck on the horses. Also she still had her thriving alterations business so they would survive, but how ironic really that her parents had forced her to marry him believing his fictional persona of a solid and upright citizen.

Lost in thought, she jumped at another knock at the door. Don't say they've come back, she thought, but it was a gentle knock not like the imperious commanding battering of before. Answering the door she was relieved to see Father Dermot standing there.

"Oh Father Dermot." Lilian breathed a sigh of relief. "I thought it might be somebody else."

"Yes, I know, I just met Maura and she said you'd had the Garda at your door. She was worried about you. Are you alright?"

"Yes, thank you, I'm fine but I did get a bit of a fright, I must say – they were rather threatening."

"To be sure, that would give you a shock but you've nothing to fear, Lilian. You've done nothing wrong."

"No, you're right, Father. Would you like to come in for a cup of tea? I think I can hear Michelle stirring from her nap."

Dermot just nodded and stepped in, closing the door behind him.

No sooner had she fetched Michelle and put the kettle on than there was another loud knock at the door. Seeing the fear in her eyes, Dermot jumped up, saying, "You stay here – I'll get it, shall I?"

"It might be…" began Lilian.

"Don't worry." He patted her hand and headed to the front door, drawing the kitchen door closed behind him.

Lilian could hear voices – men's voices – and some discussion that went on for quite a few minutes. She heard the front door close and hoped that was the end of it, but Dermot's face was grave when he came back in.

"Is it them?" Lilian whispered.

"Yes," he replied, "and they've got a search warrant. Lilian, I think it would be best if you take Michelle next door. I'll stay here and make sure they don't do any damage."

She just nodded, gathered up Michelle and went out by the back door.

Father Dermot closed the door behind her, took a deep breath and went to admit the Garda, praying a silent prayer that they wouldn't find anything incriminating.

They didn't.

Chapter 26

With Desmond away again Siobhan resumed her habit of visiting Lilian every day, always full of news and questions, prattling on and on as well as amusing Michelle a lot of the time. Lilian was then able to get on with her hand-sewing, finishing garments and sometimes mending or embroidery; she did think of bringing the sewing machine back from Maura's but decided against it, fearing that Desmond could turn up unexpectedly at any moment. It had been such a relief that Dermot had dealt with the Garda and they'd gone away without any further trouble, but Lilian couldn't escape the nagging suspicion that her supposedly respectable husband must have done something really bad this time.

One afternoon Siobhan came flying in full of excitement about the party she'd just been to, the games, the tea and the singing.

"Is Michelle going to have a party when it's her birthday?" asked Siobhan.

"Oh Michelle's not really old enough yet, Siobhan, but …… Do you know, I really love that idea. She'll be one year old next week."

"Can I come, Lilian?"

"Yes, of course you can, and Mummy and Aileen with little Liam and Father Dermot."

Siobhan jumped up, clapping her hands in glee and went over to explain to Michelle all about parties.

Lilian, meanwhile, planned in her head a simple birthday tea and a cake with one candle. Why hadn't she thought of it before? It would be lovely to have Michelle's godparents all together again and make it a little celebration. Well, the reason of course was that there was no way she could do it with Desmond around.

Lilian didn't normally make cakes, only perhaps a plain scone sometimes, but she could remember the recipe for the Victoria sandwich her mother used to often make for Sunday tea, so she borrowed some tins from Maura and set to. The cake rose beautifully and was a fairly even colour when it came out of the oven – first part of the challenge achieved.

The friendly couple at the corner shop kindly split open a pack of miniature twisted candles and sold her one for just a penny; Mrs. O'Leary then rummaged in her own kitchen drawer and produced a pretty cake frill that had only been used once.

With the cake organised, Lilian could move on to the party food – jelly for the children and paste sandwiches for the grown-ups.

Lilian had already made Michelle a new dress from some scraps of material left over from remodelling a two-piece and some spare lace, so she could wear this as her party frock.

On the day of the party Maura and Siobhan arrived first, using the front door in honour of the occasion and bearing some biscuits and a present wrapped up in brown paper. Siobhan eagerly helped Michelle to unwrap the gift which turned out to be a spinning top, probably handed down from one of the older children, but scrubbed and polished to look as good as new.

Next came Aileen with Liam, whose gift was a little rag book which Michelle looked at briefly then discarded in favour of the top; Siobhan kept both the younger ones interested in that for a while as Lilian started to make the tea. Father Dermot arrived just as the kettle had boiled and was immediately teased by the women that he always managed to appear when tea was ready. He was carrying a large and expensive-looking box. On opening the gift it contained a beautiful dressed doll for Michelle.

After tea and the ceremony of the cake (with singing) Siobhan wanted to play games so they had several rounds of 'hunt the thimble', but the little ones couldn't really get the idea and began to show their fatigue, becoming fractious. At that point Aileen gathered up Liam to go home and Dermot went off with them, both enthusiastically thanking Lilian for a lovely afternoon.

Maura insisted on helping Lilian to clear up before taking Siobhan home to stop her from playing with the new doll which, firstly, wasn't hers and secondly was much more suitable for looking at than cuddling.

Michelle, too, was clearly exhausted by the afternoon's excitement and her grand party dress showed some evidence of jelly and biscuits, but never mind, thought Lilian, it will wash out. Once Michelle was changed and asleep Lilian sank into the comfy old chair to put her feet up. The party and its preparations had provided a welcome distraction from another concern that had bothered Lilian since before Desmond went away.

This concern came forcefully to the forefront of her mind next morning when she woke up feeling horribly nauseous. She tried to convince herself that it was maybe due to the meat paste, but when it happened again the next day she couldn't fool herself any longer.

Just like the first pregnancy she felt absolutely fine after the first few days of sickness and was well able to fill her busy days taking care of Michelle and doing as much sewing as possible in order to keep up her income. It was at night, though, in spite of being very tired, that she found herself unable to sleep and worrying long into the night about how on earth she would manage to cope with another baby. She remembered so clearly Maureen's initial reaction that she'd been a fool and this time it was an accident, too, but she'd actually had no choice; Maureen had also suggested abortion, but although circumstances were this time very different, her deep love for Michelle meant she couldn't even consider it.

Sometimes she wondered what Desmond's reaction would be and the only conclusion she could come to was that he would probably blame her and be furious about another mouth to feed.

Most nights it was almost getting light before she finally slept, only to be woken by Michelle calling at her usual hour.

Even if she had felt like talking her problem over with Maura it wouldn't really have been possible, for that young woman had taken on a part-time job now that Siobhan had started school and so was always running to keep up with everything.

Maura felt she'd been so lucky to get such an opportunity which really came about due to young Sean's enthusiastic interest in wildlife: from a young age he'd always been keen on keeping various bugs in jam jars, frogs and newts in buckets, and later rescuing birds and small mammals from danger. Sometimes she'd then take them to the vet and beg his help. Thus Maura, too, got to know the animal doctor and his housekeeper. The vet was a charming man and very good at his job but rather disorganised so needed some help in taking care of his bills and invoices – the housekeeper had suggested Maura, and the arrangement suited very well.

Lilian and Aileen continued to meet up two or three times a week to get some exercise and fresh air for the children and themselves. Sitting in their favourite bench by the stream while Michelle and Liam fed crumbs to some ducklings, Aileen suddenly said, "Have you got something to tell me, Lilian?"

"What do you mean?" replied Lilian.

Aileen returned what is known as an old-fashioned look. "You're expecting, aren't you?"

Lilian nodded and sighed. "Mmm, how did you know? It's not showing, is it?"

"No, not at all," replied her friend. "It's just that you've got a sort of calm about you."

Lilian grimaced ruefully. "Not so much calm, more dread, I think."

"Why aren't you pleased, then?"

"I can't say I am, Aileen. I don't know how I'm going to manage with two and I don't know what Desmond'll say."

"Oh, come on, Lilian, you'll manage. The second one's always easier, so they say, and it'll be lovely for Michelle to have a little brother or sister. I think you should be pleased. I wish I was pregnant. Now that Donal's away it would give me something to look forward to."

Lilian knew that her friend was still upset that her husband had joined up in spite of her fears for him, so she didn't push the point in spite of the fact that she was anything but pleased.

At that moment there was a splash and a yell – Liam had gone a little too near the edge and slipped into the stream. He wasn't hurt or in any danger but he was covered in mud. Both women jumped up and ran over to pull him out, Aileen's relief spilling over into exasperation. "Oh Liam, if there's any mud and muck to be found, you'll find it. He's soaking wet," she went on. "I'll have to go straight home."

"Yes alright, see you later." Lilian couldn't help smiling at the dejected look on the little boy's face – they had been having such fun.

Chapter 27

Lilian gasped at the sight that met her: Desmond was slumped in the kitchen chair looking as though he had been sleeping rough or in a fight, or possibly both. His eyes were closed but when he sensed her entering, he opened one eye and half-heartedly raised a hand.

They'd just come in from shopping and Michelle looked anxiously out from behind her mother – he'd been away so long that she'd forgotten he used to bounce her on his knee when he was in a good mood. Or possibly she just didn't recognise him in his dishevelled state.

"Are you ill? Are you hurt?" asked Lilian.

"No, I'm just bloody knackered and I could murder one of those cups of tea that you're so famous for."

Michelle stayed warily in the corner while Lilian put the kettle on and asked, "When did you last eat?"

"Can't remember," he mumbled.

Lilian reached for her last two eggs and scrambled them to put on a piece of toasted soda bread. The man looked so awful and he was her husband after all.

Desmond fell upon the simple meal as though he truly hadn't eaten in days and when he'd finished sighed gratefully.

"Thanks, Lilian, you're a good girl."

Moments later he was asleep and showed no sign of stirring for hours. Lilian whispered to Michelle that they should keep quiet so as not to disturb him. The little girl enjoyed the game of whispering and tiptoeing around as they carried on with the chores.

In the end it was bedtime and he still hadn't risen from his slumber so she left a glass of water on the table and covered him with a blanket.

Next morning Lilian was up quite early as usual and amazed to find the blanket thrown in the chair but no sign of Desmond. Had he gone off again? What was he playing at?

Even more surprisingly he reappeared a couple of hours later, having somehow washed, shaved and acquired some neater clothes. Immediately he struck up a conversation as though he'd never been away.

What a strange man he's become, thought Lilian, but judged it best to follow his lead and not demand any explanations.

Eventually he asked, "Did you get any more trouble from the Garda?"

"They came back once and searched the house – I don't know what for."

"They wouldn't have found anything so let's hope they leave us alone now. None of their business anyway," he grunted.

While he'd been away, Lilian had been able to organise her time to work her household duties and care for Michelle around the sewing and repair business which was flourishing. Her immediate worry now was how she would be able to keep from him that she was still doing the work in Maura's front room. An idea that came to her was that she would tell him about Maura's part-time job and say that she was looking after the little one while she worked. In the event, just as before, he was frequently out most of the day and half the night anyway so she was able to carry on pretty much as before.

Lilian could hardly believe that Desmond had been back for three days and still not mentioned her very obvious pregnancy, so in the end she said to him: "Have you not noticed that we're having a baby?"

"I have," he replied sourly. "That's quite a surprise, isn't it!? When's it due?"

"In about six weeks' time. I've already booked Kitty Flaherty, the midwife and we won't need …."

Desmond loudly interrupted her. "Well, you can just un-book her. I'm not having that woman in this house – she's the biggest gossip going!"

"But I don't know of anyone else to deliver the baby and she was so good last time," begged Lilian.

"You can go and have it at the convent: that's what women usually do in your situation."

Lilian was unsure what he meant by "your situation", but she let that go, feeling more concern for Michelle.

"But who will look after Michelle if I'm away for a few days, Desmond?"

"I'll look after her or your precious friend from next door.

You're always doing things for her so she can do something in return. I'm not having that busybody in the house, and that's final!"

The raised voices had woken Michelle from her nap and she began crying, so Lilian went up to fetch her. When they came down Desmond was in the front room tinkering about with the lock on the cupboard; the Garda had broken into it when they searched and his priority was to get it fixed.

As usual, Lilian tried to carry on and keep things as normal as possible for the child, though she was still upset and worried about having to cancel the midwife and go to a strange place to have her baby.

As if she didn't feel bad enough, there was a further upset later the same day when Desmond came storming down the stairs clutching Michelle's big doll as though it was vermin. Lilian had put it away wrapped in a shawl at the top of her wardrobe to keep until Michelle was old enough to appreciate it, so she knew he had been rummaging around again; thank goodness her savings were now in her handbag in the kitchen.

"What's this," he roared, "and where did it come from!?"

"It's Michelle's birthday present from her godfather but I put it away until she's a bit older."

"Godfather! You mean that damned priest again? Talk about when the cat's away the mice will play! I'm telling you, Lilian, if I ever find him in this house again I won't be responsible for my actions!"

"Oh Desmond, it's just a doll."

"Yes and a very expensive one by the look of it."

At that he seemed to get an idea and, whereas before he'd looked as if he might throw it across the room, he now looked it over and murmured, "Mmm, must have cost a pretty penny, I should think."

Lilian reached out to take it back but he brushed her hand away, saying, "I'll look after it."

Next thing Lilian heard was the rattling of the cupboard lock in the front room and she knew for certain it was his intention to sell the doll.

After he'd gone out Lilian gathered up Michelle and went next door to do some of her sewing, partly because she had an order that she'd promised for the weekend, but also because she always found sewing could calm her. Maura was at work and not due back for an hour or so; she was well into the second curtain and Michelle was happily playing with cotton reels on the floor when Maura breezed in.

"Hello, my dears. And how's my best little girl?"

Maura whisked Michelle up for a cuddle before stopping to look at Lilian whose eyes were a bit red from weeping a few tears of anger and frustration.

"What's the matter, Lilian? Are you alright?"

"Yes, it's just…. Desmond doesn't want me to have the baby at home. He's insisting I go to the convent and I'm so worried about leaving Michelle." Maura reached out to her friend immediately.

"Don't worry about that. I'll look after her, I promise – she'll be fine but you'll have to change your plans now – cancel Kitty, pack a case and you'll need a gig or a taxi to get there – it's right on the outskirts of town, you know."

"Oh, I hadn't thought of that," sighed Lilian. "I'll have to work out about transport and I haven't really got a suitable suitcase."

"That's not a problem. I can lend you a small one and," said Maura with a cheeky grin, "there's always Mike Milligan's handcart if the worst comes to the worst."

At that, both women burst out laughing and were soon in hysterics, much to Michelle's surprise.

When they finally stopped laughing, Lilian said, "You're such a good friend, Maura, you always cheer me up."

"I've got to get the kids' tea going now so you can just carry on but really, Lilian, don't worry – we'll sort something out. I'll bring the case down before you go, though."

This baby was in no hurry to enter the world: the predicted date had passed more than two weeks ago. At last Lilian woke in the early hour to a cramp-like sensation and knew that it wouldn't be long now. By the morning the contractions were fairly regular so she woke Desmond and told him she needed to get things ready. For once he was up and dressed quite quickly but made no attempt to help her and simply said, "I've got to go out. You'd better take her (Michelle) next door."

Fortunately it was early so Maura and the children were still at home. Maura took charge immediately, giving Michelle her breakfast and sending Sean to run to the stables for a gig. When the gig arrived it was driven by the same old chap who'd met them from the station all that time ago. He remembered Lilian and was kind, taking her small case and helping her up.

Chapter 28

Lilian's heart sank as she clambered down from the gig: the convent looked like a prison, with bars at the small, sparse windows and a big old iron door. She thought she had rarely seen such a forbidding building. She paid the driver and noted that he crossed himself as he drove off.

The iron bell pull produced a deep clang from somewhere far off but the grill in the door shot open immediately, making Lilian jump. Before she could speak it slammed shut again and she could hear bolts clattering, before the small entry door in the vast portal creaked open. A young nun in the grey habit of the novice stood aside to let her in before silently replacing the bolts. Still without speaking, she motioned to Lilian to follow her and set off down the long corridor at a cracking pace, far too fast for a woman in the advanced stages of labour. At the first corner she did stop to wait for her charge to catch up, with some show of impatience. The girl's demeanour was not at all what Lilian imagined an aspiring nun to be; there was no calm serenity in her face, more a sour and hostile glare.

At last they reached the ward after passing by a cloistered courtyard which could have been quite beautiful but somehow just looked lonely and sad. The ward was a long, bare room with bare boards and about ten beds along each side. The only ornament was a small crucifix above each bed. There was a small group of young women at the far end of the room, a young girl weeping on one of the beds, and an older woman, heavily pregnant on the nearest bed. There was no sign of any babies.

The novice pointed to the next bed and addressed Lilian who had begun to think she must belong to a silent order, "Get undressed and Sister Assumpta will examine you shortly."

"That'll be nice," grinned the older woman with a sarcastic smirk. "Don't worry, dear," she continued. "Assumpta is a bit rough-and-ready but she does know what she's doing. Mind you, her favourite phrase is 'You've had the pleasure, now you have the pain'. Don't ask me how she knows anything about the pleasure!"

The woman proceeded to introduce herself while Lilian started to get changed. There was no privacy whatsoever.

"When's yours due?" asked Lilian, trying to make conversation to take her mind off the wholly alien atmosphere of the place.

Madge (as she had introduced herself) started to answer but was interrupted by a nun ringing a handbell, whereupon the door at the end of the ward opened and all the young women, except one, trooped out.

"What's that?"

"Feeding time," replied Madge. "Just twenty minutes to feed and change the babes before getting back to work."

Lilian was horrified at the regimentation, remembering how

warm and supportive Kathleen had been when Michelle was born. Sure enough, twenty minutes later the girls were roughly pushed back into the ward and quickly despatched to the laundry, kitchen or scullery. None of them looked her way but she could see that several of them had tears in their eyes.

By now, Lilian's contractions were coming thick and fast; she tried to concentrate on deep breaths, as Kathleen had shown her, but it got harder and harder. Eventually Sister Assumpta appeared and helped her to a small room, not much more than a cupboard really, with a high couch.

The next few hours became a haze of pain and exhaustion until finally the grim-faced nun wordlessly washed the squalling baby and wrapped him tightly in a rough towel before laying him in a cot prior to wheeling it to the nursery.

Lilian struggled to sit up and feebly called over, "I've got a nice shawl to wrap him in – it's in my case."

"Not necessary," replied the woman tightly.

Just then a young nun came in to take over and the older woman left. This girl looked much more human so Lilian tried again, asking to hold her baby and begging the nun to fetch her soft shawl for him.

"I shouldn't really," answered the softly spoken girl, "but I suppose it'll be alright just for a while."

Smiling and thanking the girl, Lilian took her son and checked to be sure that he was indeed a boy. Somehow she'd known that without being told. She stroked his soft cheek and immediately felt that strong bond and connection just as she had with Michelle. After a time she wondered and asked why the girl had said she shouldn't give her baby to her.

"Well, the babies are supposed to go straight to the nursery and only be available at feeding times. They say it's better that you don't get too attached to them."

Lilian heard the words but they didn't seem to make sense; she wanted to ask what on earth they meant but she couldn't seem to put her words together; her brain was too muddled and she was too tired. The young nun gently took the baby from her and a moment later she was asleep.

Some hours later, Lilian woke in the ward with the friendly face of Madge beside her. Struggling to sit up, she cried, "Where's my baby?"

"It's alright, dear, they've taken him to the nursery. You'll see him again at feeding time."

Lilian sighed with relief and smiled at the memory of his soft cheek and perfect little hands.

"He's really beautiful, Madge. I'm going to call him Andrew."

"Are you now?" replied the older woman with a quizzical look. "They won't like that."

"Who won't like that?"

"The nuns – you don't know, do you?"

"Know what? I don't understand."

"He's not yours to give a name to – he's going to be adopted – they all are."

"No! No! No!" Lilian cried, shaking her head. "He's my baby – I'm taking him home. I've got another little girl and a husband."

"You'd better see Mother Superior, then, because that's not the deal they expect."

Lilian started to get out of bed but the older woman gently stopped her, saying, "You can't go now, Lilian, you're still very weak. Wait until you're a bit stronger – he won't be going anywhere for at least a few days."

Feeding time didn't go too well as Lilian was frightened, angry and tense. The baby seemed to pick up her feelings and couldn't settle. When the bell rang to return to the ward, Lilian hadn't settled him down and she refused to leave until two large nuns forcibly took him away and pushed her out of the nursery. Still very weak, she leaned against the door in tears until another girl helped her back to bed.

Although she was still quite weak and exhausted, Lilian found it difficult to sleep that night: thoughts went around in her head of how to get herself and her child out of there and she wondered if Desmond knew what he was getting her into.

The next day and the next day she told every nun she saw that she must meet with Mother Superior: some of them smiled and nodded as if she was deranged, some just ignored her; only one said she would try to arrange it. By this time she was deemed fit enough to work and spent long hours in the kitchen or the scullery on menial tasks. In the end she realised she was going to have to take drastic action either to forcibly see this unattainable holy woman, or simply to run away and escape somehow.

More days passed and still no sign of an appointment with Reverend Mother or even a senior nun, so Lilian hatched a plan: all the nuns went to service in the chapel three times a day and the chapel was just a short corridor away from the scullery, so she would wait till they were all in there and run down to force her way in.

The plan worked like a dream – all the nuns not on duty were at vespers so she watched until the one overseeing nun was busy with something and flew along the corridor. No one had seen her, but she mustn't hesitate now, so she burst in the door and called out at the top of her voice, "I want to see Reverend Mother!"

The shock in the chapel was palpable for long moments until two traditionally built nuns grabbed her and would have pushed her out of the room but she continued to struggle and shout until a stern, elderly nun raised an imperious hand and said, "Take her to my room – I will deal with her."

Lilian's elation at the success of her plan was short-lived – replaced by apprehension as she was roughly pushed into the bare, dark room that was the Mother Superior's office and inner sanctum; what a contrast to the rich and ornate splendour of the chapel.

As soon as the service was over, the Reverend Mother swept in, her habit rustling about her. The flapping of the black veil, her angular features and cold, piercing eyes put Lilian in mind of a large and dangerous bird of prey. Even her hands, spread on the desk before her, looked like talons, though Lilian was mildly surprised to see they bore several large, glittering rings.

"You'd better explain your behaviour, young woman!" she sourly spat out.

Summoning all her courage, bolstered by the love of her child, Lilian replied, "I had to see you and, although I've asked for an appointment nobody listened."

The nun looked amazed and asked, "Why do you need to see me?" as though such an idea had never entered her head.

"I need to arrange to take my baby home."

"Don't be foolish, girl; the babies stay here until they go to the care of someone who can look after them properly."

"I can look after him," Lilian almost shouted. "I'm not destitute, I have a husband and a home and a little girl. If you don't believe me you can ask Father Dermot from the church. He's Michelle's godfather – he knows us very well."

Mother Superior blinked in disbelief and muttered, "Father Dermot, you say?" For quite some time she regarded Lilian suspiciously, before opening a large, ledger-like book and saying, "I'd better take some details so I can check out your story."

After asking Lilian all about names and dates and details of Michelle's baptism, she put her pen down and sternly said, "Go back to your work, I have to make some enquiries."

Lilian heard nothing for two more days until the young nun who had been kind to her at the birth called her out from the scullery and said, "You've to collect your things right away. I'll bring the baby and escort you to the door."

Lilian's heart was beating like it would fly out of her chest as she beamed at the young nun and flew down the corridor to the ward. It took no time at all to throw her things together. She would have liked to say goodbye to Madge, but the older woman was nowhere to be seen and she couldn't wait. Right outside the ward she met the sister who handed her sleeping child to her. As though in a dream, they set off down the main corridor to the gate. Hearing some footsteps behind her, Lilian increased her pace, not daring to look behind until she heard a familiar voice.

"Hold up, Lilian, let me carry your case."

"Dermot! It's you – have you told them?"

"Of course I've told them. Come on, let's get you home."

Chapter 29

When they arrived at the house Lilian was excited and apprehensive in equal measure: excited to see Michelle and show her her new little brother, apprehensive about the reception they might get from Desmond. He'd been surprisingly good with Michelle when she was a baby, though, and surely any man would be happy to see his son. How could she possibly have imagined the greeting she would get?

Lilian rapped three times on the knocker – not too hard – rocking the baby while they waited, for he was becoming fractious near to feeding time. No sound came from the house; perhaps he was out. Lilian knocked again a bit louder and the door flew open as if he'd been standing right behind it. Jumping back a little, she exclaimed, "Oh, I thought you were out!"

Desmond glared at the little group on the pavement, his eyes narrowing as he spat out, "What do you want?"

Puzzled as she was, Lilian held the baby towards him, saying, "We have a baby boy, Desmond."

"He's no child of mine!" shouted Desmond. "Clear off and take your fancy man with you!"

Lilian and Father Dermot were both speechless, the implication clear that Desmond thought the priest was the baby's father.

Dermot partially recovered first and suggested they go next door to see if Maura was in. Maura had in fact heard the kerfuffle and peered through her front room curtains, so opened her door even before they knocked.

"What's going on?" were her first words. "Come in, Lilian, you look done in."

Nudging the door wide open she held out her arms for the baby and stood back to let them in.

"Oh I can't stop," muttered Dermot, "I've got to get ready for Mass," and off he hurried, looking rather sheepish.

"What's the matter with him?" asked Maura but didn't wait for an answer before ushering Lilian to a chair.

"Right, now I'll make a pot of tea and it looks like this little fella's ready for a feed."

Siobhan came peeping round the door when her mother was in the kitchen.

"Can I hold your baby, Lilian?"

"Not just at the moment, poppet, but you can hold his hand while he feeds."

The baby curled his fingers around one of the little girl's fingers and Siobhan beamed happily at once.

Maura brought in the tea and poured two cups. She could see that Lilian was only just holding back the tears so she asked Siobhan to fetch the sugar bowl from the pantry, though she knew full well that neither needed sugar.

Lilian understood at once that this was her cue to confide in her friend and she wasted no time. "I think he's gone mad, Maura. He wouldn't let me in – he told me to clear off – he thinks the baby's not his – and I haven't seen Michelle! Is she alright?" By now tears were pouring down her cheeks and the baby had stopped feeding and started to yell. Even though Maura had never any time for Desmond, she could hardly believe what she was hearing.

"Come on now, Lilian, try and calm down or you won't be able to feed your little one. Michelle is alright, I've seen her and I've minded her a couple of times – don't worry. If you like I'll come with you to see him again."

"No, it's better if I go by myself. Would you look after the baby?"

"Of course, but drink your tea first."

Screwing up her courage, Lilian again knocked on the door, a bit harder this time. He took ages to answer: she could hear bolts being drawn and locks rattling like it was a fortress.

"You again!" He snarled. "I thought I told you to go away."

"Listen to me, Desmond – you've got it all wrong – the baby is yours. Now please let me take Michelle next door – she'll want to meet her little brother."

Desmond laughed scornfully. "Do you really expect me to believe that? You seem to forget I know you of old – now sling your hook, the kid stays here."

With that, he reached behind the door, grabbed a bundle of clothes, threw them onto the pavement and slammed the door.

Lilian threw herself against the door, hammering with her fist and weeping. "Please, Desmond, please, let me see Michelle." She'd almost sunk to the ground when Maura came out, baby in one arm, to help her back indoors.

After she'd coaxed her to sit down and handed her the baby, who was miraculously sound asleep, Maura dashed out to retrieve the clothes from the pavement.

"Oh, thanks, Maura. What am I going to do?"

"You're going to get yourself fit and strong again before anything else. You'll be no use to either of them if you collapse. Now I'd be happy to have you stay here but to be honest, Lilian, I think it's better if he doesn't know where you are."

Lilian sighed and nodded.

"I think I could go and stay with Aileen – she's got plenty of room with Donal away."

"That's what I was thinking. He doesn't know where she lives, does he?"

"No. I'm sure he doesn't. I'd better make a move," she continued, starting to get up, "before it gets dark."

"You stay there and rest a bit; I'll send Sean for the gig. No, wait a minute, I've got a better idea: Mr. O'Leary at the corner shop has just got himself a little delivery van, that'd be quicker and more comfortable. I'm sure he'll help when I explain the problem."

"Don't tell him he's thrown me out, Maura."

"No, I'll just say you've got to go and stay with your friend and you're only just out of bed."

O'Leary actually wasn't keen and complained that he had to use his petrol ration for his business, not on errands of mercy, but Mrs. O'Leary, up to her elbows in pastry in the back kitchen, overheard and bustled out to berate her husband soundly:

"Patrick O'Leary, you get yourself out to that van right away and give that grand little girl a lift. I don't know what you're thinking to put your petrol ration above a small favour for a really sweet girl!" She was still brandishing her rolling pin so Patrick shifted pretty quickly, muttering, "Sure, I was only saying that petrol's limited… O.K. I'm going, I'm going."

At Aileen's house the kindly grocer helped Lilian out, carried her bags and waited to see that someone was home. Aileen was most surprised to see a delivery van at her door and even more surprised to see her friend looking so wretched. It was quite clear the girl was exhausted so she drew her in without delay, took the baby and made her rest in a soft armchair. Small talk was easy – cooing over the baby – so she chattered on a while, waiting until Lilian felt able to partly explain her appearance and her problem.

"Of course you can stay – it won't take a minute to make up the spare room – I'm afraid I've moved Liam in with me since Donal's been away. Now when did you last eat? You look all in."

"I can't remember," answered Lilian, smiling weakly and reaching for the baby who'd started to stir.

"Right, I'll fetch out the baby crib for him and then a warm plate of colcannon has got your name on it, Lilian."

"Thanks, Aileen, you're so good."

When at last the two little boys were both sleeping soundly, Aileen and her guest sat down by the fire with a pot of tea and before long Lilian poured out the whole sorry saga, from Andrew's birth at the convent to the surreal shock of being thrown out by her husband. It was only when she began to speak about Michelle that her hands began to shake so much that she had to put her cup down.

"He's got Michelle, Aileen. I've got to get her back – I've got to."

Aileen rose to comfort her friend and to calm her, the best she could. "We'll go back there tomorrow, Lilian. I'll come with you."

"But what?" sobbed Lilian. "What if he won't give her up?"

"Then we'll go to the Garda – that'll soon frighten him. Come on now, let's get you to bed. I daresay you'll be up in the night to the little one, so you need some sleep now."

Lilian didn't expect to be able to sleep but in fact her emotional and physical exhaustion was so great that she slept almost as soon as her head hit the pillow.

In the morning she didn't wake until the baby started whimpering and Aileen came in with a bowl of porridge and a tray.

"Oh Aileen, you do spoil me."

"High time someone looked after you," replied her friend. "Now, when you've finished with the babe and your breakfast you stay and rest a while. You've got to get your strength back after all you've been through."

Lilian smiled ruefully. "That's just what Maura said."

"Yes, there you are, then. Listen to your Auntie Maura," laughed Aileen.

"I've got to get up, though," objected Lilian, "so we can go back round to the house." Saying this, she swung her legs out of bed to stand up but promptly felt so weak and dizzy that she had to sit back down.

"One more day won't make any difference. You're going to rest today," said Aileen firmly.

In the event it was another two or three days before Lilian was really up to the walk to the other side of the village. Even then she was a bit shaky but refused point-blank to wait any longer. Aileen wheeled out Liam's pram, glad that she had kept it, although her son no longer needed it. They tucked Andrew up inside, sat Liam at the front and set off.

By the time they arrived at the house Lilian's heart was pounding and she was as white as a sheet. Aileen tried to smile reassuringly as she stepped up to the door, but in truth she was pretty nervous, too, knowing the reputation of the man from years ago. Lilian knocked tentatively and they waited. No sound.

Aileen gently nudged her aside and knocked herself – much louder – then she bent down to peer through the letter box and finally into the front room window.

"He's not there, Lilian, but look, here comes Maura, maybe she knows something."

Maura was just coming back from her job at the vet's and greeted her friends with mixed feelings as she had really no good news about Michelle: the house had been quiet most of the time and she'd seen neither Desmond nor the little girl. As they drank tea in Maura's kitchen she explained all this and sadly agreed with Aileen that the only thing to do was contact the Garda.

"How do we do that, then?" sighed Lilian.

"Well, we'll need to go along to the station," replied Aileen. "But you're not up to it today. We need to get home for a rest and we'll go tomorrow."

Lilian was reluctant to leave it another day but both her friends convinced her it would be best.

At the Garda station next day they were seen by a plump, jolly-looking officer, nothing like the two who had called on Lilian before. He took down all the 'particulars', as he kept saying, and kindly assured them that he would pass the information on.

"I'll have to give all these particulars to my s-o-o-periors," he said with great emphasis, "and we'll let you know in due course."

For several days they heard nothing. Meanwhile, Lilian trekked up to the house whenever she could, but to no avail.

It was early evening when a loud, official knock at the door made the girls jump. There stood one of the sour-looking Garda who had searched the house some months ago. Aileen was in two minds as to whether to ask him in or risk the neighbours seeing him at the door. Thank goodness Donal's not here – he'd be furious at having the Garda on his doorstep, she thought. She didn't like the look of him anyway, so she called Lilian and the two women stood together in the doorway.

Lilian's heart was in her mouth and she could hardly believe the information he relayed which was that because Mr. Blackstock was her legal husband this was merely a 'domestic' matter and no crime had been committed.

Chapter 30

The news that the Garda couldn't or wouldn't help to find Michelle left Lilian bereft and desolate. She began to spend part of each day wandering wraith-like around the area in the hope of catching a glimpse of her daughter. Sometimes she'd return to the house, too, but it was always locked and silent.

Maura and Aileen were at a loss as to how to get their friend back on track: they tried persuading, they tried bullying, they did manage to get her interested in some more needlework assignments but she couldn't concentrate properly and they didn't go too well.

Aileen, in particular, couldn't help wondering how long she was going to have these two rather demanding house guests; Lilian was paying her way a bit with the money from sewing and her savings, but if Donal should get leave she didn't expect he'd be very pleased. Fortunately little Andrew came up trumps with the magic of his first smile: it got through to Lilian as no one else had been able to and led her at last to begin to think about his future and her own.

The evening routine of feeding, bathing and bedtime was over when Lilian and Aileen sat beside the fire for a quiet cup of tea.

"Aileen, it's time I decided where to go from here. You've been so good to us, but I've got to stand on my own two feet sometime."

Aileen nodded. "What will you do?"

"I think I'll go back to England – I'm not really doing any good here. But I'll come back whenever I can – I'll never give up searching for Michelle."

Her friend sighed and smiled as she anxiously bit her lips.

"Will you go back to your parents?"

"Oh no! I don't think I can ever go back there again."

"Why not? Did you have such a falling out?"

"Aileen, they virtually forced me to marry Desmond just for respectability, and apparently they even gave him money to bring me here. I'm finished with them."

"Well, what then?"

"The only thing I can think of is to take up my old job managing the bookshop and live in the little flat above. It's not ideal because it's quite close to my parents but I don't know what else to do. I'm going to write to Albert and ask him – I know he'll help if he can."

"Albert – that's your old boss, is it?"

Lilian nodded and the two sat quietly with their own thoughts for a while.

"By the way," said Aileen, "on another matter altogether, I bumped into Father Dermot earlier and he was asking after you and the baby."

"Oh, was he? It seemed to me he's given us a wide berth after Desmond's vile slur, and is thinking only of his holy reputation, no doubt."

"That's tosh, nobody's gonna believe that nonsense – he's well respected and so are you."

"Well, you know what people say – no smoke without fire."

Aileen laughed, then continued, "Well, anyway, he asked if you'd thought about having Andrew baptised – have you?"

"No," said Lilian thoughtfully, "but I suppose I ought to. Shall we go to church together on Sunday and see about it?"

"Sure – I think it's a good idea."

At church several of the congregation, mostly elderly ladies, greeted Lilian and cooed over the baby. Lilian had learned from Maura how to take part in the service and some of the Latin responses, but this time her heart wasn't in it. She simply gazed at the crucifix and the stained-glass windows, having a feeling of numbness from within.

After the service Father Dermot immediately came to find them to arrange the baptism – ever eager for new recruits.

"It's good to see you, Lilian," he began. "Aileen told me your husband has Michelle – I'm sorry to hear that. She is always in my prayers."

"Thank you, Father. Now about the baptism – it will have to be quite soon as I'm planning to go back to England."

"We can do it next Sunday after the service if that suits."

So that was arranged and they set off home. On the way Lilian said, "I'm going to write to Albert this afternoon and post it straight away."

After lunch Lilian spent quite a while composing the letter: she wrote about the baby and the break-up of her marriage, before broaching the subject of the shop, and took care not to sound too desperate. Aileen had a spare stamp because she always kept some ready to write to Donal so Lilian was able to go straight out to post the letter. She dropped it into the letter box with a silent little prayer and on the way home felt calmer than she had in weeks.

Albert must have read between the lines of her letter because a reply came almost by return containing not only an offer of a position, but also enough money for the fare.

Apparently the shop had been sold, as Albert never intended to return to it and, although his health was much improved, he found himself in need of a live-in housekeeper.

The letter was warm but formal, offering help with no strings attached. With a deep sigh she handed the letter to Aileen who had been eagerly watching and showed her the money.

"Well, that's good news, isn't it?" said Aileen, handing the letter back, surprised that Lilian didn't seem pleased.

"Yes, I suppose so."

Both knew the problem was that she'd be leaving without her daughter but neither spoke about it.

The next day was Sunday, the day Andrew was due to be baptised. Aileen kindly lent the lovely christening robe that had been Liam's and they set off to church with Lilian fervently hoping the baby wouldn't be sick on it. Mr. and Mrs. O'Leary had delightedly agreed to be godparents and they met at the church.

The baptism was short and sweet, for this time the baby didn't cry at all.

There was no party but Dermot accompanied the girls home for a cup a cup of tea. Lilian then told him of her plans and he kindly offered help in arranging tickets and some accommodation on the way.

"You'll need to stay over in Dublin. I know a lovely family who'll look after you and get you to the ship. I'll get in touch with them tomorrow and check on times of trains and sailings – you don't need to worry about anything."

Lilian gratefully accepted his help and he went off in good spirits, glad to help.

In far less time than she'd thought possible, the arrangements were all made and Lilian wrote to Albert to tell him she was on her way. With a heavy heart she sorted out and packed her few belongings and what she needed for the baby.

Maura and Aileen accompanied her to the station and the train was on time. After tearful farewells and promises to keep in touch, she boarded and found a space in the first compartment. The other passengers consisted of an elderly lady, a smartly dressed gentleman, and a young boy in a posh school uniform. The man kindly put her luggage onto the rack and she sat down where she could see her friends to wave goodbye.

As she looked out, Maura started to point frantically towards a commotion at the station gate. Wondering what was going on, she peered along the platform where she saw a young priest, cassock flying, carrying a child, running towards the train. She jumped up, thrust Andrew to the lady, saying, "Please hold him for a moment," and ran to the carriage door. Father Dermot was able to pass Michelle to her just as the whistle blew and the train started to move.

"Where did you find her?"

Panting hard and gasping for breath, Father Dermot managed to say, "He took her to the convent for adoption. I only just found out."

"Thank you, thank you, thank you," she called as the train drew away, the priest waving in a way that showed he was sorry to see her go.

Lilian hugged and kissed her precious little girl, unable to believe her joy. The child looked well and happy, dressed in a neat little coat and sturdy shoes.

Back in the compartment, quite unfazed, Michelle sat on her mother's lap and gazed out of the window as the verdant countryside whizzed by.

"Where are we going, Mummy?" she asked.

"We're going home, sweetheart, we're going home."

Don't Dunk Your Biscuits